Murder in Monterey

MURDER IN MONTEREY

OR

DEPUTY MARSHAL

ERIC PATRICK DANIELSON

ARCHWAY
PUBLISHING

Archway Publishing books may be ordered through booksellers or by contacting:

Archway Publishing
1663 Liberty Drive
Bloomington, IN 47403
www.archwaypublishing.com
1 (888) 242-5904

ISBN: 978-1-4808-1709-8 (sc)
ISBN: 978-1-4808-1710-4 (e)

Library of Congress Control Number: 2015904740

Print information available on the last page.

Archway Publishing rev. date: 6/10/2015

To Mike Lee and Dennis Blain

PART ONE

THE RENTED RANCH HOUSE

I

It was June 1970. Dell Sandberg walked into his rented house on a beach north of Seaside, California. The house had a cabana that looked out over the Pacific. Dell splashed scotch into a glass. He preferred bourbon. Mabel would arrive at five, and they would have dinner. Hank Swanson and his press card would arrive the next day.

Mabel knocked right at five with her luggage and a typewriter for Dell.

They dined on TV dinners Dell had heated up, and they sat in the cabana, drinking whiskey sours.

Dell was a private agent and a freelance writer for a magazine back east. Salt Lake City was his hometown, and Mabel was a friend who worked with him and Hank.

Evening settled over central California. They drank a few more whiskey sours before turning in at ten.

"Good-night, Dell," said Mabel from the doorway.

"Good-night, Mabel." Dell was thinking about the summer. Their plans were set. "If all goes well, I'll have a publisher here in Monterey," he said.

"Yes," said Mabel. "Someone should give you recognition to your work. I wish you the best with your publisher." She headed to the guest bedroom.

Mabel disappeared. Dell ground out a cigarette, went inside, and locked up. He was soon sleeping soundly.

The next morning, Dell plugged in the typewriter. He started working on an article on Indochina. At two in the afternoon, he walked on the beach to a bar not far away. He ordered a beer, which a nice-looking cocktail waitress brought to him. He smoked, and he drank his beer slowly. At three, he left a good tip and headed back to his house. He could hear booms coming from the firing ranges at Fort Ord, just to the north.

He saw Mabel and Hank in the doorway. Hank was of medium height and heavily built. Mabel was a petite brunette, while Dell was proud of his height. "Hello, Hank," Dell said.

"Hello, Dell."

The three entered the house, and Hank sat. He had driven three hundred miles that day. Mabel brought them beer. "Good evening, the two of you," she said.

The three chatted. It was the year before that they had made plans to spend the summer in California.

"Enough of work," said Mabel.

Hank talked easily. "I had a job back east that lasted until Christmas. I photographed several big cities and won an award."

"I'm here to see quite a prolific West Coast editor," Dell said. "I'll see him tomorrow."

Hank applauded Dell. "You're writing for several magazines, aren't you?"

"Yep," was Dell's reply.

They dined on TV dinners while watching the news and discussing it. They settled into the cabana, where Dell nursed a beer. At ten, they all turned in.

Dell woke up the next morning and figured Mabel and Hank had gone somewhere. He cooked an omelet and made coffee. After breakfast, after a cigarette, he got to work on his article on Vietnam, which Phil Burt, editor of *Argo's* magazine, a flesh magazine and journal, was paying $1,000 for. Dell had an appointment with him at two that afternoon.

After working a few hours and having a quick lunch, he drove to his appointment and got there five minutes early. The suite outside of Phil's office was swarming with women in bathing suits. Phil was in his office decorated with covers of his porn publications.

"Mr. Philip Burt, California millionaire."

"Mr. Dell, freelance writer."

This was the extent of their introductions.

Dell handed Phil his article, "The Cretins of Indochina."

Burt told him he'd have a check for $1,000 in a few days. He invited Dell to a party the following Wednesday, five days away. "Be here at seven," Phil told him.

Dell left and drove toward Seaside but stopped at a bar, where he drank beer for the rest of the afternoon. He got back to his place at six, and he, Mabel, and Hank had more TV dinners and spent the evening drinking in the cabana.

It was time for bed. Friday evening came to a conclusion.

On Wednesday night, Mabel and Hank were watching TV while Dell got dressed for the party. Dell liked girls, and Phil was a gracious host.

Dell, who had gotten the $1,000 check on Monday, learned from Phil that Dell's article was coming out at the end of the month.

On Thursday morning, Dell entered the cabana and got to work on an article that was going to cover the stupidity of Indochina. By the afternoon, he had produced ten pages and figured it was time for a beer. Mabel had done some shopping, so there was beer in the fridge. Dell popped a tab and took a good gulp. He stripped to take a shower.

Mabel and Hank wanted to go out to dinner, so Dell was ready by five. They went to a German restaurant in Monterey and were back by seven. Whiskey flowed in the cabana, but Dell stuck with beer. The three were partners. They drank to success.

On Friday, Dell stopped at Phil's office to sign a receipt for the payment. Phil wasn't looking very well. There had been too much wine, women, and song at the party two days earlier, and Phil's head still ached.

Dell was back by noon, and Mabel made lunch. Hank was out taking photos. Dell and Hank worked together; Dell was the journalist with a degree, and Hank was an excellent photographer.

Dell got back to work on his article on Vietnam and finished it by six. He enjoyed relaxed California evenings. A cool breeze came off the ocean as he mixed drinks for Mabel and Hank and popped a top on a beer for himself. They celebrated Dell's completion of his article.

The following Saturday night, they had no plans but to drink what Mabel had bought at the liquor store. They talked, smoked, and drank in the $1,000-a-month beach house that was theirs for the summer. Dell planned to return to Salt Lake City in the fall, so he was drinking in the California summer on the beach. One might have thought a war was not taking place on the other side of the ocean.

Phil called Dell about another article he wanted about Indochina for another thousand. Burt didn't say why, but he had been pleased with Dell's first article.

Dell set to work on an article that would cover the pros and cons of the Vietnam War. Personally, he was pro Nixon and in favor of the war. He already had a title for this next article: "The Auspice of Indochina."

Dell and Hank had served in Korea. Both were dogfaces who had plans to become journalists after the war. Dell had attended the University of Utah, while Hank had attended the University of Minnesota. Mabel had attended a junior college linked to New Mexico State. The three were excited about a second article in *Argo's*.

Dell drove his second article over to Phil and received his second thousand-dollar payment. *Argo's* was going to host another party on Thursday night that Dell planned to attend. He was pleased.

He stopped at the Seaside Hotel for some beer but was back to work by the afternoon. Hank and Mabel had spent the day touring Monterey, but the three were together that evening. The next morning, Dell set to work and typed all day. "I'm working on an article on the promising military situation," Dell told Mabel and Hank.

"Yes. Things look promising. I think we're in a good position," Hank said.

The war in Vietnam seemed to be at stalemate after bitter fighting in the earlier years. Dell was basing his article on that.

Thursday evening came. Dell attended the party at *Argo's* and was again surrounded by beauty.

"What are your views on Vietnam?" one guest asked Dell.

"Nixon has the right idea," someone said.

"I don't agree," said the first guest in a very businesslike manner.

Dell let them debate the matter. He was more interested in chatting with a beautiful woman and drinking.

Dell woke up Friday morning with a hangover. He promised Phil a pro-Nixon, win-the-war article that was to be ready by July 4. He popped open a beer. It took the edge off his hangover, but his stomach was queasy. Hank was up. Mabel got up.

For some reason, beer was what they all needed that morning for breakfast. Dell showered and changed into clean clothes. Hank wanted photos of the Fourth of July celebration in Monterey. Associated Press paid him for his photography on the home front, and he wanted to shoot the antiwar movement stateside. Dell got to work on another article for Phil. He was looking forward to another *Argo's* party Monday night.

Dell hammered away at his typewriter in the cabana until two that afternoon. He stubbed out his cigarette and took a hike to the bar on the beach. The waitress served him beers, which he drank slowly. He headed back at five.

He reread his intro to "The Auspice of Indochina." Phil endorsed Nixon, so Dell was sure this article would please him even though most of *Argo's* writers were liberal intelligentsia. That evening, they drank and watched TV.

The aircraft carrier USS *Ticonderoga* was scheduled to visit Monterey Bay during the Fourth of July week, having just gotten back from a tour of Yankee Station off the coast of Vietnam. The ship's air crews were veterans of combat missions over North Vietnam. Hank wanted photos, and Mabel would assist him.

Mabel was scrambling eggs for breakfast one Sunday when they caught some news on TV. A girl's body had been found near Monterey. She had been stabbed multiple times.

"Check this morning's paper," Hank said to Dell. "Any clues there?"

Dell scanned the paper. "It's a drug murder. She was in a commune near Fort Ord. She went missing Thursday night. She was found dead late last night."

They finished breakfast, relaxed, and had an early dinner that afternoon at the German restaurant. They learned no more about the dead girl.

On Monday morning, Dell was busy typing and taking breaks for beers. The murder, of course, was still in the paper. The police interviewed people at the commune but had made no arrests.

Dell's July 4 deadline was approaching. Hank had taken many shots of the USS *Ticonderoga* in port. He had photos of thousands of sailors back from the Gulf of Tonkin and a thin line of protestors who had peacefully formed up along the harbor. Many were from the commune.

Dell attended another *Argo's* party. Phil was pleased with Dell's article on Indochina. He mentioned that the dead girl in the paper had been one of his girls the year before, which was news to Dell. Phil thought that a pusher could have killed her.

Dell had introduced Mabel and Hank to Phil at one party, and Phil was impressed with Hank's photography. He offered Hank a thousand dollars for his portfolio of Monterey shots, which pleased Hank.

After a Monday-night party at *Argo's*, Dell woke up and threw up. He downed some beer as the hair of the dog. Hank was hungover too. The two drank all morning. The newspaper reports on the murder had died down, but it was still on Dell's and Hank's minds. They wondered about the commune, and they wondered if the girl's murder was somehow linked to the drug dealing they knew was taking place at *Argo's*. They knew Phil sold drugs and porn along with his magazine, and they thought Phil could have been involved in the murder.

Dell retrieved his shotgun from the trunk of his car and put it in the cabana. Phil published nude photography and controversial magazine articles and sold thousands of magazines on the West Coast. He was widely known for the belligerent attitude his magazine took. That the dead girl had been one of Phil's bathing beauties the year before looked like it could be a break in the case. The sting operation had aimed at indicting Phil on interstate racketeering charges, but Dell, Hank, and Mabel thought they could possibly get him for murder as well.

The three were undercover US marshals. That was why they attended Phil's parties.

One morning, Mabel came into the kitchen for some coffee. Dell was there, battling another hangover. He had had two articles appear in *Argo's* and had earned a grand each, and Hank had earned some for his photography, but they had to keep up their cover. After a few hours in the cabana, he headed down the beach for a beer.

At one party they attended at Phil's, they witnessed some of the partygoers indulging in cocaine, but the three kept their identities to themselves. They were feds seeking information on Phil. Drugs were one thing, but murder was another. The three were deep in thought as the evening settled over Monterey.

Frank Elder was a Mormon bishop and a US marshal with jurisdiction in California. A year previously, he had cracked a drug smuggling ring in Utah as head of a federal task force on the war on drugs. His deputy marshals were Dell and Hank, and Mabel Martinez was a Salt Lake City policewoman.

Frank called Dell with a warning to stay undercover. "Be quiet." Dell knew what that meant. The trio of deputy marshals kept low profiles.

The July and August 1970 issues of *Argo's* offered two prominent articles, one pro and the other con, on Southeast Asia, both written by Dell, himself a hawk. At that time, US troops were withdrawing from the invasion of Cambodia, and Richard Nixon was promoting his ideas on the Vietnamization of the war. He was still noting the use of cocaine and the nude girls at Phil's parties. The atmosphere was left wing, but Dell received praise for his writing. Many doves thought Dell would come around to their way of thinking. "You are young, sir," said a Monterey businessman in between snorts of coke.

Dell, Mabel, and Hank were more interested in the drugs and what they thought was prostitution going on at Phil's than they were in their articles and photos. The girl who had died could have been one of Phil's prostitutes. Dell, Hank, and Mabel were working on the case that probably involved murder.

"When will you be back in Salt Lake City?" Frank asked Dell during one call.

"After Labor Day."

That was his deadline to wrap up the case. Maybe he could write more for *Argo's*.

Dell had met Katie Bewell at one of Phil's parties and was going to escort her to another. "Be sure to wear a two-piece suit," implored Phil. Katie was rich girl, and everyone wanted her money. She cast looks at Phil. Dell told her he would be ready by seven. It was August. Summer was on the wane.

Katie picked up Dell right at seven and complimented him on his article on communism. "That was well written," she told him.

One Saturday morning, Mabel and Hank were drinking coffee while Dell was smoking. He walked to the beach bar at ten for a beer. It was a little early to drink, but he was happy with the money he had earned from his writing. He had an article coming out in the magazine in early September. He considered himself lucky, but then he thought of the murdered girl who used to live in that drug-ridden commune. He thought locking up Phil on drug, prostitution, and murder charges.

Dell sat and drank beer as he waited for Katie to pick him up. Hank and Mabel spent their time exploring Monterey. Hank had contacts in the underworld, and Mabel was an expert on prostitution.

Katie picked him up at six, and they dined at an Italian Restaurant, enjoying spumoni for dessert. When Dell got home, Hank and Mabel were watching TV. Mabel had heard that a couple of sailors from the *Ticonderoga* had visited Salinas and had gone back to their ship. Dell was interested. He jotted down the information. He watched the news before going to bed. A couple of sailors from the *Ticonderoga* were a clue. He mentioned this to Mabel.

Frank called McDuff, US marshal, federal court, San Francisco. He wanted Sam to reinforce his US deputy marshals in Monterey. McDuff was glad to oblige.

McDuff arrived at the beach house and bellowed, "Who's in charge?"

"I am. Welcome," Dell said.

McDuff told them they had until Labor Day to wrap up their investigation.

Dell explained to McDuff that a number of sailors had been in Salinas the weekend of the murder of Danielle Philips, the young girl from the commune. Dell had learned that three sailors from the *Ticonderoga* had been apprehended in San Diego.

By Labor Day, Dell had submitted his article to Phil. "Good luck," Phil had told Dell. "Send *Playboy* your next article."

The parties were over for the summer. Katie and Dell said their good-byes. The trio of marshals wondered what they had accomplished.

McDuff returned to Stockton. Hank and Mabel drove to Los Angeles. Dell headed to Salt Lake City.

It was October, and Dell sat with Frank in a bar on 21st South in Salt Lake City. The two were drinking beer. Frank had gotten Dell's report. Their sting hadn't stung anyone.

"What do you think?" Dell asked.

"He's deep into cocaine," Frank said. "I see here you got the name of his pusher. What do you know about Chico? And what was the name of the dead girl again? Was she a hooker?"

"Danielle Philips. Her parents live in Palo Alto. She was eighteen. How far does Phil deal the cocaine?"

"All over the West Coast," Frank said.

Dell whistled.

"You did your job. Did Phil suspect you're a deputy marshal?"

"Nope."

"Well done. I want you to crack this case. Burt also deals in grass and prostitution, and I want you to find this girl's killer. Can you go back to California?"

"Yes."

"Rent that beach house again, through Memorial Day. You're a federal sting operation. I'll notify the FBI. Good writing, by the way."

Dell had his orders. He would see Katie again. He planned to leave the next day for Monterey and pop the top of a Coors when he got to the beach house.

Katie swung her slender legs over the mattress and pulled on a shirt. Dell lay in bed. "Where does Phil's cocaine come from?" Dell asked her.

"Why don't you ask the cops?"

Dell got back into the habit of writing. He was working on another article for *Argo's*. He would head to his beach bar in the afternoon for three or four beers and be back at the house by five or so. Katie would come around six, and they would have dinner.

Dell and Katie attended a magazine party one Thursday night with the usual results. Dell woke up in desperate need of a beer before getting to work. He planned on seeing Hank and Mabel around Thanksgiving, but meanwhile, Katie was his liaison to Phil, whom Dell badly wanted to indict for racketeering, drugs, prostitution, and the murder of Danielle Philips.

The three sailors from the USS *Ticonderoga*, back from the Vietnam War, were on trial in San Diego for Danielle's murder. Korea had been Dell's war. The Red Chinese had attacked in overwhelming, human-wave assaults, and Dell remembered the furious fighting. He thought it was critical to contain communism and didn't agree with the general antiwar sentiments.

Dell kept on frequenting the beach bar, where the waitress knew him well from the past summer. Dell smoked and drank. He thought of three sailors. The police were not certain if they were guilty even thought they had learned that Danielle had bummed a couple of smokes from them. Dell wasn't sure if they had the right suspects. Her boyfriend in the commune was also suspect. Dell finished his beer and left a good tip.

One Tuesday night, he and Katie went out. Though Dell would ask questions about Phil's activities, Katie was silent about him.

"Is he a broker for street drugs?" Dell asked.

"That could be true."

"Is he a front for the mob?"

"I'm not certain."

"What did Phil have to do with Danielle?"

"Phil had nothing to do with her. He regrets her death."

Katie knew nothing about the death. She couldn't recall anyone interested in Danielle. "Maybe some local creep killed her."

All she knew was that Dell was a talented writer. "Treat him well," Phil had told her.

Dell and Katie kept attending parties at the magazine, at which beer, booze, and cocaine flowed freely, as did the girls.

McDuff stopped by to see how Dell was doing. Dell reported on Phil's obvious and deep connection to the cocaine trade. McDuff said he'd report to Frank. "Do you need help?" McDuff asked Dell.

"Hank and Mabel are coming up around Thanksgiving."

"I'll contact the local police," McDuff said. "A squad car will assist you."

"Yes sir."

"Do you want to charge Phil?"

"Not right now," Dell said. "I want more information."

"Very well," said McDuff. "I'll be in touch with Elder about all this."

Dell worked on his article for *Argo's* in between attending the cocaine and booze parties at the magazine with Katie. Phil continued to get praise from the liberal intelligentsia he met there; they liked his writing, if not his politics.

Dell knew Phil was a front for drugs and prostitution; that was evident from the parties he threw, and Dell had been to plenty of them.

"Are you a cop?" Katie finally asked Dell.

"Yes."

Dell had Phil's blessing for another article on Indochina. In the meantime, Dell was given the name of Chico Gonzales, who handled the more furtive aspect of Phil's enterprises. Dell quivered a little bit as he made note of Chico. Chico was a pusher. He supplied the cocaine to Phil's parties. He might know who killed Danielle Philips. Dell thought this. He was more than sure of it.

5

When Hank and Mabel drove up to Monterey on the tenth of November, Dell welcomed them. He brought them up to speed on his investigation of Phil but reported no progress on the murder.

"Three sailors are on trial for murder in San Diego," said Dell. "One of the sailors carried a buck knife."

"We should go back to that commune again," said Hank. Mabel agreed.

"Who is Chico Gonzales?" Mabel asked Dell.

"He's the man behind Phil," Dell said.

"When are we going to arrest Phil?" Hank asked.

"Wait and see," said Dell.

Dell sat in the beach bar and counted the familiar faces. The bartender asked him where he was from, and Dell said, "Salt Lake City." He went over in his mind what he knew. Chico supplied Phil with cocaine and could have been involved in Danielle's murder. Danielle's commune boyfriend was also a suspect.

Life went on for the trio of marshals at the beach house through December, and Dell was busy writing for the magazine. His most recent article on Vietnam had earned Phil's praise. Dell was turning into a prominent writer.

"What does Hank do in his spare time? Is he the fuzz?" Phil asked Dell. "Chico's my friend, but I'll admit he's an underworld type. But *Argo's* is a clean periodical that sells journalism and sex. A little dope and lots of whiskey are mixed in at our parties, though," Phil said.

Dell and Katie attended a Christmas party at which Dell was surrounded by bathing beauties. Phil liked Dell and was glad for their mutual success—four articles in four issues. Dell was becoming a writer of some merit on Southeast Asia.

Katie drove Dell home. She said goodnight and left him at the door. Hank opened the door, and Dell saw Mabel drinking scotch in the kitchen. Mabel pressed a can of beer into Dell's hand. "Congratulations, Dell," she said.

They stayed up to watch Alfred Hitchcock. They all realized Chico was the man they needed to address.

On Christmas, the three marshals exchanged gifts. Hank received an electric razor. Mabel had a new skirt and blouse. Dell had a carton of cigarettes. The turkey was cooked by one that afternoon, and they sat to eat and enjoy drinks after dinner. The three laughed and enjoyed Christmas Day.

Katie stopped by; she had been to Phil's for Christmas. She invited Dell to a magazine party on New Year's. Dell was busy planning another article for *Argo's*. He had a title: "An Honorable Peace," and Phil wanted it by May.

"You're good business, Sandberg, but I still don't follow you," Phil said.

Dell knew his status at *Argo's* was at a height. They had five months to clinch the sting, but the marshals still had so many questions and not enough answers.

The next day, Katie was found dead in her apartment.

6

"Who are you?" Phil asked Dell. "Are you a cop? Katie mentioned you were."

"Yes, I'm a cop," Dell said, but he didn't go into details about his being a US deputy marshal or what he was investigating.

"I thought so. You're writing is good, but I figured you for a fed."

"Yes sir," said Dell.

"We're looking at another murder," said Phil. "First, there was that commune girl, and now one of my current models. Any idea who might have killed them?"

"I'd like to talk with your supplier, Chico."

"Very well, and I want you to investigate these murders, Sandberg."

"Yes sir," said Dell.

"A goddamn fed," Phil exclaimed.

Dell returned to his place, vowing to find the killer or killers. Hank and Mabel were there, and Frank called. Dell told him about Katie's murder and that he wasn't sure if there was one killer or two or how they were connected to Phil. He explained he was zeroing in on Chico or someone else who attended those wild parties at Phil's. He said he was sure the murders were connected.

On a Wednesday night, Dell went to a magazine party. As usual, cocaine and whiskey were in abundance. Word went around that he was a fed. Dell said no more about his status as a cop as he mingled with the other guests. He saw Chico, and Phil came over to introduce them. "Chico, Dell."

The two shook hands. But that was it. Dell headed home, leaving behind all the businesspeople, other writers, the gorgeous women, the booze, and the cocaine. Katie's death had affected him. He had a beer, an American beer. Other countries had beer as well. That made them friendly countries in Dell's mind.

The next morning, he had a beer for breakfast and got to work on his current article, "An Honorable Peace."

Blue Smith, the county sheriff, had been assigned to Dell by the auspices of Jim Bowdoin, a homicide detective with the Monterey police. Blue knew of the murders in his county. He and Dell and McDuff, who had come for this meeting, held a council of war; they drank beer as they strategized their approach to the investigation.

Jim, who was working under the assumption that the murderer lived near Carmel or Monterey, believed the murders involved drugs, but he didn't know if they were dealing with one or two murderers.

The others at the council filled Jim in with the details of the federal case.

"We're working a sting on Phil," Dell said. "Both girls were connected to Phil, and they both used drugs, which were readily available at Phil's parties. Chico Gonzales is the supplier."

Jim said that he'd look into Chico, but Dell thought there could be another player involved, someone also connected to the magazine. Dell was happy to have the extra help Blue, McDuff, and Jim were offering. The four of them sat back and stacked up beer cans. Dell set aside his thoughts on the article he was working on and turned his thoughts to the murders. They needed answers to their questions.

Phil asked Dell to come to another party at the magazine, and Dell, of course, went, always curious about whom he'd meet there. Dell didn't think *Argo's* was involved in racketeering; it was just another nudie magazine. But he did figure Chico, or someone close to him, as their prime suspect.

Jim had talked to Chico, who swore he was innocent of anything and didn't know anything about the murders.

When Phil learned that Jim had spoken with Chico, he asked Dell, "Is he the FBI?"

"Narcotics enter this?" Blue asked Del and the others.

"Yes," said Dell.

"Phil, this is your investigation," Jim said.

"I want to wait until Hank and Mabel get back from San Francisco at the end of January. They're conducting some undercover narcotics investigations there, and they might have come up with something," Dell said.

"How was your trip?" Dell asked Hank and Mabel when they arrived at the house. Hank had photos for Phil. They had posed as a couple from Haight-Ashbury.

At a meeting with Blue, Jim, and the other new team members, they talked about Danielle and Katie. "Phil has asked for our assistance with finding the killer or killers."

"What are we looking for?" Blue asked.

"A connection to that commune, which is called the East Commune," Jim answered.

Homicide investigators had found a footprint near where Danielle had been killed, and they had found what looked like a matching footprint where Katie had been murdered. If they had come from the killer, he wore a size-eight shoe and was a small man, in Jim's mind, who wore Wellington boots. They were searching for a connection between the homicides and the narcotics, and Dell noted that Chico wore dress boots.

Dell decided it was time to visit the commune and Danielle's boy-friend in Salinas, and Jim would have another with Chico.

The team was about to run across another player, Mark Jacob.

8

Dell sat in his bar on the beach. He had been out to the commune, near Fort Ord, and had talked to the man who seemed to be in charge. But he didn't learn anything he hadn't known before. She had left Thursday night and had been found dead Saturday morning in a ditch.

Dell attended some of Phil's parties in February. Phil asked him if *Argo's* was on the federal government's radar, and Dell affirmed that. Phil was silent. Dell was welcome at his parties because he was a good writer for *Argo's*, a nationally ranked nudie magazine that paid good money for articles, especially about the Vietnam War.

Dell focused on Chico, definitely an underworld type, a pusher who snorted cocaine himself at the parties, but it wasn't clear he was involved in the murders. Dell turned his attention to Mark, a slight young man who wore boots. He catered the parties; he came with the booze and the sandwiches.

"Check him out," Blue told Dell.

In February 1971, South Vietnam invaded Laos. The war was real if not solely an American endeavor. Lives were still being lost. Dell attended a magazine party one Friday night and met Candy McBride, another of Phil's girls. Dell wondered if he could get any information out of her about Phil and his magazine.

A week passed, and Dell was going to another party. Mark was his suspect, but they still had Chico under scrutiny as well. Dell spent time with Candy at the party, which was in full swing. Dell had the chance to mingle with Mark even though he was surrounded by girls. Phil drew

Mark into a conversation with Dell. "Dell here is a federal marshal who's investigating *Argo's*," Phil said.

The party surrounded him, and the topic of conversation turned to Vietnam. "I read your article in the July issue," one guest said. Many of the people who attended the party knew he was a fed.

Dell looked at Mark and Candy, who were talking with each other. He knew she felt apprehensive about the murders, as did all of Phil's girls. "Mr. Burt was good to them," she had told Dell as she dropped him off at his place.

Dell explained the situation to Hank, Mabel, Jim, and the others on their team. "Chico supplies the cocaine for Phil's parties. But is Phil involved with the mob? Chico says that Phil doesn't get involved with the mob. He told me he handled the more-furtive aspects of his enterprise."

Candy picked him up Tuesday night for a party at which there would be a prize for the best nude photo of the girls. "What about the seedy side of your enterprise?" Dell asked Candy. She knew nothing of that. "Danielle Philips had been a prostitute," Dell said, but Candy said she knew nothing about that either, and Dell believed her. But he wondered if the drugs went from Monterey to San Francisco and then to LA. He was sure Chico was involved in this, but he wondered how Mark and Chico operated.

Dell thought of the commune he had visited the previous Friday, but after Blue told Jim, "That commune is in my county," they agreed to leave the commune for Blue. He was busy investigating local drug circles while Jim handled the murder investigations.

One Monday night, Candy swung by to pick up Dell. She had been a centerfold for *Argo's* and had received $5,000 for the photos. Candy became an instant celebrity.

Dell wondered what she could tell him about Mark.

"He caters parties all around here," she told Dell. "And he likes all the girls at *Argo's*. His whiskey and caviar are great, and he does good business."

At the party, Phil announced, "Mr. Sandberg is a federal officer looking for wrongdoing here."

People laughed and commented on Dell, who remained affable.

"We're a nude periodical that offers good nonfiction," Phil continued.

Candy drove Dell home, and they agreed to go out the following Friday.

Inside, Blue gave Dell a beer and the team watched TV. But Dell still wanted to learn more about Chico and Mark. Much more.

PART TWO

EASTER

9

Heather Dandelion was the proprietor of Good Look Modeling Academy in Monterey. She was a strict disciplinarian, and she remembered Danielle and Katie.

"Yes, my graduates go to Phil to pose nude," she told Dell. "But I don't advocate nude modeling."

Dell thanked her for her time.

He and Jim grabbed a bite to eat before heading home. They talked about the modeling school and how it could be linked to the murders. Dell had not told Heather he was a US deputy marshal.

Heather had been a guest at several of Phil's parties to see her girls and to learn that Phil appreciated them. In spite of the fact she did not advocate nude modeling, she told her girls to work hard and pose well for *Argo's*. The competition she faced in the modeling school business made her happy her graduates could find work at *Argo's*. She knew Dell as writer who attended Phil's parties.

Phil wanted the killers found and arrested. He said he was worried about which of his girls could be next.

The three sailors from the *Ticonderoga* were found not guilty. The blood stain on the buck knife had come from cleaning and dressing fish. This was the testimony of Seaman Martinez. Dell spoke to Martinez.

"She bummed a couple of smokes from us," said Martinez, "and then we returned to the ship by bus."

Martinez didn't remember meeting anyone else from the commune and knew nothing about Katie's death. He didn't know anything about Danielle being a prostitute.

Dell represented the establishment. For good or bad, oppressive or not, capitalistic or socialistic, he represented Uncle Sam and believed in due process.

That evening, Dell and Candy mingled at a party. Dell was dressed in a worsted-wool jacket. He happened to mention narcotics.

"Are you FBI?" people asked.

"No, I'm a federal officer," he answered.

They talked about Vietnam. "It's a maze of complications and misunderstandings," said a group. "You present a good war," someone told Dell. "Why don't you settle down and make a name for yourself?"

"I could establish myself, as it were," said Dell.

People laughed.

Dell drank a beer while Candy nursed a drink. They were home by ten. Candy kissed him good night. He noticed that she wept. She was silent.

McDuff arrived from Stockton and wanted to know any new developments. Dell could tell him little other than the two victims had both been models at the Good Look Salon. "Heather's in business with Tory Anderson, a dancer at the school. They've been in business for ten years. No mishaps until now."

Jim said, "I learned that Danielle Philips had thumbed a ride to Salinas."

"How was her day in Monterey? Where'd she go on Friday?" Dell asked.

It turned out that the people in the commune said she had stayed at an acid pad.

Jim visited a few drug types in Monterey and Salinas, trying to find out what he could about Katie, while Hank and Mabel were continuing to investigate Phil and his business. Blue mentioned that Pat Jorgenson, a narcotics detective with the Monterey police, might be able to help them.

After lunch one spring day, Dell walked along the beach to his bar, where he drank and smoked and thought about his responsibility as a deputy marshal. He wondered what Frank thought about the murders and the cocaine at Phil's parties. Was Phil involved in the murders? No answers. Dell left the bar at five.

At a magazine party he and Candy attended, he spoke with Mark. Phil approached him and asked him about how the murder investigation was going.

"Drugs are involved," Dell said. He headed home.

10

Dell typed away in his cabana.

> In August 1964, two US destroyers, the *Maddox* and the *Turner Joy*, were cruising the Gulf of Tonkin off North Vietnam. In the south, a battalion a week of South Vietnamese troops were being destroyed by the Viet Cong. South Vietnam was falling. Ho Chi Minh and the National Liberation Front ruled the country north of the DMZ, the dividing line in Vietnam.
>
> In August, North Vietnamese torpedo boats assailed the *Maddox,* and the *Turner Joy* was sent to assist. The *Maddox* opened fire with its five-inch guns. Four North Vietnamese torpedo boats were sunk.
>
> That attack prompted Congress to pass the Gulf of Tonkin Resolution. President Johnson asked Congress to intervene in the struggle in Indochina with troops. This was the opening of the Second Indochina War.

He was working on his article "An Honorable Peace" and explaining the purpose of the United States' intervention in Vietnam. Dell was described the war. In the bloody fighting and Laotian neutrality with Cambodia stability and peace were the underlying reasons for the loss of life. Indochina stood as an entity defying the Russian Revolution and the I Ching of Ho Chi Minh.

In 1965, a half-million US troops were committed to South Vietnam. Off the coast of North Vietnam, the US 7th Fleet, at Yankee and Dixie Stations, launched their aircraft with orders to bomb Hanoi; Haiphong, a deep-water port in the Gulf of Tonkin; and the Red Chinese island of Hainan, off the coast of North Vietnam. Diplomacy prevented the Red Chinese from interfering as they had in the Korean War.

The French had colonized Vietnam since 1840 and had gotten all the way to Cambodia and Laos by the twentieth century. Hanoi was the capital of Indochina, while the old imperial city of Hue was south of the DMZ.

France fell to the Nazis in 1940, when Japan emerged as an imperial power that quickly occupied French Indochina, whose position between the Pacific and Indian Oceans was of strategic importance. After Japan attacked Pearl Harbor, it invaded the Far East and conquered Malaysia, the Philippines, and Dutch Indonesia. The Japanese army invaded Burma. But after the Battle of Midway, which cost the Japanese four aircraft carriers, Japan was forced on the defensive a sea. The US industrial power was unleashed.

After the war, France once again administered Indochina. Two dictators arose, one in North Korea and another in North Vietnam—Kim Il Sung, and Ho Chi Minh, both Marxists. East and West met in the Cold War; the Soviet Union and Red China had world conquest in mind. But in the West, Europe and North America withstood the Communist bloc. The Cold War became a hot war in French Indochina and South Korea.

Korea's Kim Il Sung attacked South Korea, and North Vietnamese forces defeated the French forces in 1954 at the battle of Dien Bien Phu. Though they were defeated in battle, the French did not abandon Indochina. Royal and conservative factions in the south of the country did not accept the Viet Minh north of the 17th parallel.

Thus concluded the First Indochina War and French colonial rule in Indochina. The region was divided into Laos, Cambodia, and North and South Vietnam. The Viet Minh, staunch supporters of Marx, controlled North Vietnam. South Vietnam was to be governed by popular rule and democracy.

Dell wrote this in the cabana at the rear of the house. The ocean washed the shore only a few feet away. It was a cool, raw March on the Monterey peninsula, but Dell knew the season would change.

Dell wrote about how the Second Vietnam War was considered by some to be a civil war, but others looked upon it as a battle between Marxist and Western values. Dell favored the Republic of South Vietnam.

He and Candy were planning on attending a magazine party, and he was sure he would receive compliments on this article, "An Honorable Peace." But Dell was still focusing on his undercover assignment, and he was focused mostly on Chico. Dell's thoughts never wandered far from Phil, a multimillionaire with plenty of influence and women but who kept a low profile and seemed to work only a few hours a week. Phil was a monolith. He was at the center of many things going on in central California. His *Argo's* magazine was an organ of dissent as well as a venue for photos of nude women.

Dell drank beer. He liked to drink beer, but he never got drunk. He considered beer to be wholesome and medicinal, as opposed to drugs. He watched his drinking because Candy was under his protection. Dell wanted Jim to keep an eye on the Good Look Salon and Heather.

"We'll see what happens this summer. We're dealing with sedition and murder," McDuff told Dell.

"I have a feeling this will all come together in the strangest way," Dell said.

"Anything new, Detective?" the bartender at the beach bar asked.

"Just two killings," Dell said.

At the house, Blue was drinking beer while Dell was mashing what seemed to be hundreds of empty cans. Mabel was out buying more beer and TV dinners.

Mabel returned, a can of beer in her hand, just as Dell was heading out to a magazine party with Candy, who was waiting for him in her car.

"Who's your girlfriend?" Candy asked Dell.

"A friend."

"Tell her to be careful."

The remark registered with Dell. "I will."

Dell didn't think Mabel was threatened, but he planned on telling Hank.

The main office at the magazine was flooded with gorgeous women in bathing suits. Mark was serving drinks to a crowd of guests that included some actors and actresses as well as the usual business types. They could smell marijuana and see people doing cocaine.

Dell stuck with beer while Candy drank a daiquiri. They saw Heather arrive with Tory, her dancing partner at the salon. Heather asked for a gin and tonic.

Heather steered for Dell amid so many business suits and bathing suits with a Pabst Blue Ribbon for Dell. "Enjoying the party?" she asked.

Dell was indeed enjoying himself. Candy stood a few feet away. People were snorting cocaine and smoking grass. Chico was at work distributing his products, ten dollars a lid. Crumpled tens filled his pockets.

"What are you thinking, sir?" Chico asked Dell.

"Do you drink?"

"Yes I do," Chico said. "I like gin."

"Any women with you?" Dell asked.

"Just myself and my old lady."

"Do you carry a knife?"

A knife suddenly appeared in Chico's hand. He snapped his wrist. A lock of hair flattened against the blade. The knife disappeared. Dell was sure he was short a lock of hair. He realized Chico didn't play games. The two laughed.

"A good conversation, Mr. Sandberg," Chico said.

Dell left him with his paper bag full of cocaine. He finished his beer, took Candy's hand, and headed out to her car. She reminded him to look after Mabel. He said he would.

Mabel was asleep. So was Hank. Blue was smoking. Jim lay quietly on the living room couch, watching TV. Dell shook Mabel awake.

"Be careful, Mabel," Dell said.

Mabel rolled over and opened her eyes. She was a pretty brunette.

"Yes, Dell," she said. She rolled over and went back to sleep.

Dell headed to his room.

Dell woke the next day just slightly hungover. Jim and Blue were already up. Hank and Mabel came in, beers in hand. Mabel said she'd make lunch.

The morning passed. Dell remembered what Chico had said. He remembered his stiletto. He listened to Iron Butterfly's "In A Gadda Da Vida" as he thought about Chico.

Jim killed another brew. He was in charge of protecting Good Look Salon and Heather, and he considered the models as his charges as well.

Dell cast a protective eye at Mabel. Hank and Mabel had been to LA and Frisco and had posed as a couple in Haight-Ashbury.

"Chico is well heeled," Dell told Jim, who was getting pressure from his department to solve the murders. Dell still didn't think Phil was involved.

After lunch, Jim drove to a VIP's for some coffee and some thinking about the murders. He thought about how Katie had been alone in the early morning. The killer got in. She was dressed. People knew little and would tell them even less. Silence reigned. The local police could piece together only so much.

Back at the beach house, Dell offered Jim a beer. Nothing had gone on that afternoon. Hank and Mabel had been quiet. Dell had cleaned his service revolver and was doing his laundry while drinking beer. This was a homicide investigation, after all. Dell filled another plastic bag with empties.

Evening gathered over Monterey. In the distance was Carmel. Dell wondered where Chico could be found after hours. Dell was surprised by Chico. He did not menace people. He was a businessman even if he was selling something illegal.

12

Mabel went out to shop for beer and TV dinners. "Budweiser," Dell had told her. They drank Bud. Blue was sprawled on the couch all morning. He watched TV. He waited for the evening news. Dinner was going to be at five.

They drank beer. Their beer bashes served as a cover for their police activities. Hank and Mabel were in and out of the house. Jim was working on the homicides, and Blue was protecting his county. Dell kept an eye on *Argo's* but didn't feel he had enough evidence for an indictment.

Mabel served TV dinners at five. Blue was keeping an eye on the news. "South Vietnam is invading Laos. Some young South Vietnamese general was killed. There's heavy fighting going on."

They all wondered if the South Vietnamese could take over the war, as President Nixon wanted them to.

"The North Vietnamese occupy part of Laos."

At seven, they watched Muhammad Ali fight Joe Frazier.

"I give it to Frazier," said Jim. "Ali will be back."

They stayed up to watch Alfred Hitchcock and drink beer.

Saturday morning came. Dell was the only one up. He made coffee and smoked as he waited for the others to stir.

He donned a sports jacket and headed for downtown Monterey. He sat in a tavern and ordered a beer. The bar was quiet. Two woman came in for drinks. Dell glanced at them but said nothing. At two, the three of them left. Dell was home by five.

He had nothing to say about the scent of perfume on him except that he had driven two women to their hotel.

Mabel eyed Dell. "You were supposed to go drinking and overhear people's conversations."

Dell acknowledged this. Mabel was silent.

"Where did you go?" Hank asked.

Dell grinned and said nothing more.

Dell had been gone all day while the posse had drunk beer and played gin rummy.

"How many beers did you have?" Hank asked.

"Four," Dell said.

"That commune near Salinas harbors cocaine," Hank said.

"There was cocaine being used this afternoon," said Dell.

"Good work," Mabel said.

"Chico traffics in the stuff," Dell said.

"Drugs are prevalent," said Hank.

"It's called the East Commune," Dell said. "They grow vegetables, raise rabbits, and believe in peace."

"They aren't under surveillance," Jim said.

"Danielle Philips left the commune Thursday night. No clue to her disappearance but her bereaved boyfriend. She spent Friday in Monterey and was found dead Saturday night. Three sailors saw her. She bummed a couple of smokes from them," Dell said. "Danielle was a model and singer from the streets of Monterey."

The next morning, Dell heard the booms coming from Fort Ord as he walked to his beach bar. The cocktail waitress smiled.

"Hello. I haven't seen you in a couple of weeks."

"Business kept me busy. Hello." Dell grinned.

She served him a beer, and he lit up a smoke.

"That'll be a dollar," the waitress said.

Dell handed her a dollar. He pulled on his beer. He liked Bud. Two singles lay on the table by the ash tray. He sipped and smoked while she served other Saturday-morning customers.

Dell drank until two, left a tip, and headed home. Blue and Jim had gone out for coffee. Hank and Mabel were watching *High Chaparral*. The

Apaches were raiding the ranch. Mabel had already gotten beer and TV dinners. It was a lazy Sunday afternoon.

Blue and Jim smoked and drank coffee at a VIP's. Jim was a college grad who had worked homicide and had become a top detective. Blue, the county sheriff, was a former army warrant officer with a degree in police science. Together, they worked to resolve the homicides. They were looking for a rich bum.

Back at the house, Jim gave Dell his thoughts on the matter as they drank. Hank and Mabel discussed their plans to follow Chico and get some photos of his activities.

The evening drew to a close. Blue pulled guard duty. He checked the windows and doors front and back. Everything was secure. He sat in an armchair and dozed until six, when Dell got up to make coffee.

It was a misty morning in late March. Jim and Hank and Mabel were asleep. Dell took over for Blue. He sipped his coffee and smoked.

The household awoke about nine. Mabel came into the kitchen after her shower, and Dell poured her some coffee as she lit a cigarette.

"Let's get a bottle of gin for Chico," said Dell.

Hank and Mabel agreed. Blue and Jim smoked.

At eleven, Hank and Mabel headed out in her VW to Monterey. Jim opened a beer. Blue and Dell followed suit. They played cards. They were Confederates. They were Union troopers. "We'll see Hank and Mabel in a week," Dell said.

They sat around, waiting for developments. But they thought Phil was not dishonest.

"I'll stay home and guard the fort," said Dell. He retrieved his shotgun from the cabana.

Jim and Blue left for coffee and were back by eight that evening.

When they came in, Dell raised his weapon. "This is a guard post," Dell said to Blue, who relieved him at guard.

The week passed. The following Monday, they heard Mabel's VW. Dell presented arms with his riot gun again.

Phil glowered and scratched. His porn empire was intact. He kept it clandestine to avoid society's sanctions and the wholesome American way of life. He was antiwar. So many kids were being blown to pieces in an impossible, public, political fiasco. He thought they should fight the Russians and Red Chinese. *MacArthur was right,* he thought. *They should bomb a billion Chinese with Fat Boy and Little Boy. And you can add in two hundred million Russians who served that Doomsday machine.*

He wrote a nationally syndicated column, and he paid a thousand for articles on the dispute in Indochina, pro or con. He was commercially sound.

He knew that Dell wrote well with insight, even though he was a conservative. Phil liked journalists who provoked readers into bringing policy out of mayhem. The conflict in Indochina was a strategic issue to world diplomacy in his mind. He had voted for Nixon and considered Humphrey a fool. He thought that liberals were simple, kind-hearted idealists, while Nixon represented power, money, and reality. He wanted the South Vietnamese to fight their own war.

He arose at seven and showered, finishing off with a blast of cold water. He shaved and brushed his teeth. He combed his hair and put on a shirt, tie, and jacket. He critically evaluated himself in the mirror. He would pass. He put on dark socks and highly polished shoes. He looked every inch the businessman.

He lived alone. His wife and children lived in Sacramento. He ate some cereal and drank coffee before leaving for work in his economical Toyota. His magazine took up a big business suite in Monterey, while his magazine design studio was in Fresno. He also had a porn studio in Monterey.

He arrived at work at eight, as did the rest of his staff, thirty people and about two dozen girls. Another dozen girls were on call as necessary. He paid good money for his services.

Phil went over the proofs for the upcoming issue. He reread the articles and checked the photos as he drank coffee. He looked over the advertisements before he signed off on the issue and had it shipped to the printer's.

His grandfather had been a successful business manager for Levi Strauss, and his father had made his first million at age twenty by growing rice on the American River delta, something new. Phil had bank accounts in California of course but also in Nevada, in Reno, where he'd gamble, watch the shows, and relax. But the account involved money that crossed state lines, and the feds could consider that racketeering, he knew.

He'd owned *Argo's* since 1965. His magazine had grown, building a reputation for great photos and compelling articles. He owned interests in other flesh magazines and was doing very well for someone in his early forties.

He considered Dell an alcoholic, and he thought it was good news, not bad news, that Dell was a federal agent in spite of the cocaine that was so prevalent at Phil's parties. He thought Dell could solve the murder cases. He didn't think any harm would come from the grass and coke consumed at his parties, but he was afraid of the murders.

Phil decided to commission another article from Dell, this time fiction. He'd pay the author two thousand. He wanted to give the rising young writer a challenge.

Phil took his sack lunch into the lounge. He dined on an American cheese sandwich with mustard and a Coke and finished his meal with some cookies. Most of his employees went out for lunch, as they were free to do. Some would return smelling of booze. Phil noticed who was high, but his magazine sold sex, and that meant that he had had to gather an eclectic bunch of creative talent to produce it and the fashion magazine he was also working on.

Phil also owned a restaurant, a high-end, classy steak house in Monterey. All his businesses were doing well. His taxes were paid. He was a successful entrepreneur.

He went to his restaurant nightly, where the manager waited on him personally, making sure his scotch was perfect and his steak was cooked to order. As the owner, Phil didn't have to pay, but he always left a good tip for his server.

He would head back to his magazine's offices on nights he was hosting parties there. They always started at six thirty and ran to midnight. Phil enjoyed his parties. Those who attended did so for the social exposure they received. Most considered Phil's invitations to be mandatory. Phil would get home after midnight but was always up by six, ready to work.

Dell stopped by for the meeting with Phil.

"Come in," said Phil. "Thanks for coming. I want you to write a fiction article for the May issue." Phil liked getting right to the point. He poured Dell some coffee. "How's your investigation coming?"

"Chico and Mark are my two suspects. But I'm also looking into Heather."

"Keep on it, Dell."

The interview was over. Dell left. Phil remained. He drank more coffee. He enjoyed coffee. He thought of Dell, the fed.

Not long after that, he reached for his sack lunch. He ate lunch. He didn't smoke. Phil was a dove.

Frank and Amanda Halladay, a fellow Mormon and US marshal, were staring at their pitcher of beer at the Beehive Bar and Grill in Salt Lake City, on 21st South, one day in April 1971. He had gone over Dell's reports about Phil being a powerful businessman suspected of racketeering and having mob connections. Dell could prove drugs and though he could prove prostitution. Dell was up to his ears in trouble in California, not having come up with charges that could stick. But McDuff was backing Dell. "Sandberg's learning Monterey," he had told Frank.

"They know what they're doing," Frank said to Amanda, who sipped her beer. The Mormons forbade alcohol, but Frank absolved her and himself.

"It's just hops," Frank said.

"And tobacco is just an herb," she said as they puffed on cigarettes.

Frank was a Jack Mormon, that is, a Mormon who didn't follow all the dictates of Mormonism; he was a worldly US marshal. He asked Amanda what she thought was going on in California with the two murders. He knew the word was that Phil was linked to high-end prostitution and drug trafficking and had the power to twist the arms of state. His own state and other states.

"I want you to contact Dell and have Swanson and Martinez drive to Fresno."

Amanda finished her beer.

"Another thing. I want Dell to solve this murder and indict Phil."

Frank finished his beer. He liked Amanda, a good deputy.

He smoked another cigarette. It was late afternoon, and they could leave for the day. Business was done. Amanda had to return to federal district court. She had her instructions. Frank prepared to return home.

"Get on this, Amanda."

"Yes sir." The brown-haired Mormon girl smiled.

The two left. When Amanda got back to the courthouse, she phoned Dell. "Hank and Mabel have business in Fresno," she said. "Sit quiet, Dell."

Dell hung up and looked at Mabel and Hank, who was asleep on the couch. Blue and Jim were out for coffee again. Dell drank beer. He was relaxing that April day. Hank and Mabel were ready to depart the next morning.

Blue and Jim returned from VIP's. "What do we have?" Blue asked.

"Frank gave us his approbation," Dell said. "He wants Hank and Mabel to continue their work in Fresno."

"We have so many ideas," Blue told Dell.

"Work on them," said Dell. "I've heard from Frank." He did not divulge what Amanda had said in regard to Phil.

He kicked Hank awake and told him the assignment. "Frank wants you to drive to Fresno. That's where Phil's porn studio is."

Mabel was up and listening. "We'll leave by eight, and we'll be back by May first," she said.

"Good." Dell planned to inform Amanda and Frank.

It was pouring rain outside, but the weather was warmer. They popped the tabs on five cans of beer, and Mabel heated five TV dinners while Dell discussed his fiction.

At Amanda's call, the five sat and ate five hot TV dinners. The team watched the national news about the fighting in South Vietnam, and then they watched *Hawaii Five O* while drinking more beer. Nothing of importance had happened since New Year's.

Blue had ceased his surveillance of Mark, having found nothing out of the ordinary. Dell thanked Blue for his efforts.

The next morning, Hank and Mabel were showered and dressed by seven. Their bags were packed. Hank had a .38 revolver in his waistband. Mabel was armed as well.

"Fresno," said Dell. "Frank wants you to check into a few things.

Candy has explained Burt's apparatus in full. You may look into this as well."

"Fresno," said Mabel. She grinned. Hank said okay. They were on the road by eight.

Candy picked Dell up that evening for a magazine party. Dell gave Chico a pint of gin. Candy smiled at Dell. Dell marveled at Phil. *Argo's* was a fashion magazine. Heather ran a reputable modeling school. In the whole thing there was a sump.

"Is there a fashion store in San Francisco?" Dell asked Candy.

"I know one called Mayflower Fashion," Candy said.

They were looking at all of Phil's enterprises.

"I'm scared," said Candy.

Dell thought of murder. The fashion models were vulnerable at *Argo's.*

There was live music at the party. Phil played the role of host to the hilt. Models abounded. There were a hundred guests. Journalism and Indochina were the main topics of conversation. Phil advocated civil conformity and peaceful dissent. The intellectuals debated what the Cold War was all about.

At home that night, Dell digested what Candy had said. The next morning, he checked on Phil's film studio in Fresno. All was in order. Phil had a business license for the place.

There were five models since the previous July who had been threatened by homicide. Jim was given the assignment of protecting the girls. There was a killer at *Argo's,* and Dell worried about Candy and Heather.

Chico was a thirty-five-year-old dope peddler. He lived in a one-room apartment on the edge of Carmel with his old lady, Thomas. With his natural son Jesus he also had two other children. They were Thomas.

He made money hustling, and he had known for months that Dell was a cop. Chico wondered how much Dell knew, because he always seemed so reserved at Phil's parties. He expected to be arrested for cocaine dealing at the parties at some point because his dealing was so obvious, but he was sure Dell was more interested in the murders.

Chico was doing good business selling cocaine at the parties. He had bought some angel dust at the East Commune that he sold at the parties. He didn't know and didn't care where the people on the commune had gotten the stuff; he just wanted to make quick transactions, in and out, so he could sell.

He was home from the parties at midnight and up at six to make breakfast for Thomas and the kids. When Thomas went to work, he drove the kids to school, knowing a friend would drive them home after school.

He thought of the parties at *Argo's*. Phil had told him he could use him, and Phil was an important businessman who had some shady businesses. Chico stayed at home in the early mornings and watched TV and drank coffee, waiting to be contacted by his associates and start dealing around noon.

He drove to Salinas and met Babe Rhubarb. He gave her money, she went to the commune, and she came back with a pound of cocaine. Chico could sell a pound a week at the parties. Chico did his business in full view of Dell at the parties. He figured Dell was government and would remain government, but he wondered how long he could get away with dealing.

Chico liked gin and club soda with a twist of lemon. He didn't snort cocaine; that was for his customers, so many of whom were from the Monterey area. He was reasonable with them. He would charge them for drugs and give them comfort, solace, and serenity. He kept an impassive face. He thought he was liked. He was never harsh with anyone. That's how he did business.

Life was good. He had gin and soda at midnight, and Babe Rhubarb was his girlfriend and business partner in Salinas. He also sold grass to a few acquaintances; that was his bread-and-butter money. A lid went for ten bucks, and he would sell it outside a high school in Monterey that let out at three in the afternoon. He'd be home at four and ready for Phil's parties at six to sell pot and snow. He pulled in a thousand a night.

He had known Danielle. She had bought acid from him. Chico figured her boyfriend had killed her. And Chico had liked Katie. He always knew he would see Dell at the parties drinking his goddamn beer while Chico mingled and dealt. Business was good.

Phil was a celebrity in Monterey; his parties were always successful. Well-to-do couples in search of coke, grass, alcohol, and live music sought invitations to them to mingle with the magazine's writers and artists and the businesspeople and intellectuals who always showed up.

Candy pulled up in her '70 Maverick to pick up Dell. They left Jim and Blue at the house. Hank and Mabel were in Fresno.

At the party, the two mingled. Dell drank Pabst. Clouds of cigarette and grass smoke filled the room. Burt reigned as models posed for the party. The guests chatted away. As Dell spoke with Mark, he saw Chico, who was well liked by the girls though he was quiet and shy.

Dell ordered a beer. Mark handed him one. Phil walked by and smiled at Dell.

Dell was home by ten. Candy told him goodnight and promised to call him when she got home so he'd know she was safe.

Jim watched TV. Dell sat down with another beer. He stood guard with his riot gun.

Blue examined his notes he had collected on the murders. He and

Jim were convinced they were dealing with a single killer. He imagined a rich punk who had taken two girls for a ride. He was sure of this. But he wondered when it would all come together. They were all sure that narcotics was involved, but they waited for Hank and Mabel to return with information.

It was ten at night. Blue drove Dell's car on his evening patrol. He protected the people at *Argo's*.

Dell stood guard, drinking beer. When morning came, it was raining. Dell put coffee on and smoked. He lit a cigarette. He let Blue and Jim sleep.

At ten in the morning, Jim took the riot gun from Dell and sat at ease. He drank coffee. Blue awoke. He showered and changed into his sheriff's uniform. Dell went to sleep.

Blue and Jim played cards, drank beer, and smoked. It was a spring morning. The two shuffled the deck and thought of nothing in particular. They had a suspect.

Blue filled his notebook with details, but he had seen nothing unusual. Jim was an expert and he noted the forensics. Fresh face was a killer.

Dell awoke at noon. He had nothing new to report about the parties. He was hoping Hank and Mabel could turn up a new angle in Fresno that would connect with Phil, who was still at the center of the case.

Dell went back to sleep but was up at five. He showered and got dressed. He checked his wallet and saw a twenty. He decided to go out.

He walked in the drizzle to the beach bar, where Bobbie served him a beer with a smile. Dell smoked and drank beer in the uncrowded bar until eight, when he went home to take over guard duties from Jim and Blue.

They drank more beer. Dell was half drunk. Blue and Smith were the same.

The night was dark and rainy. Blue went out at eleven to check on Candy. Mark, their surveillance had concluded, was at home. Jim slept.

16

Heather sat by her phone. The thirty-seven-year-old brunette thought of *Argo's* magazine. She remembered that five years back, Phil had asked her to send over a dozen models to pose nude. She had been aghast. Her models at Good Look Salon were good girls.

"Send over a dozen," implored Phil.

She had asked her models for volunteers, and a score went over to *Argo's*. Phil paid Heather a hundred thousand dollars. That was the beginning of Good Look Salon. She ended up signing a contract with Phil to supply him with girls, who appreciated the business, and the magazine, Phil said, took on a "Grecian" air—it became classy thanks to Heather's girls.

She was committed to her business with Phil, and she became a drill instructor for her girls. Her school's regimen was severe. Her girls wanted to be models, and she put them through their paces for their work at *Argo's*. She and Phil worked well together. Though she was a Catholic who attended Mass on Sundays, she had lost her scruples about nude modeling, which meant good money.

But the murders had scared her. She remembered Danielle, who had been a prostitute and drug addict at age nineteen. She had been one of her girls who had posed for *Argo's*, as had Katie. Her death at New Year's had prompted Heather to encourage Phil to go to the police. Phil had informed her that Dell was with the feds.

Heather looked at the time and noted that it was four, time to get ready for one of Phil's parties. Tory, her partner, was coming by at six to pick her up.

At the party, Phil kissed her hand. He was surrounded by a dozen models. Heather went to Mark for her customary gin and tonic. She was wearing a stunning fur cape. Tory was her escort, but Phil was her paramour.

Dell and Candy showed up at the party, where everyone enjoyed the live band, the HoneyBees, with a female vocalist. Dell and Candy watched Heather and Tory leave at nine. Dell made conversation and drank beer. He and Candy left at ten.

Candy dropped him off, and Dell said goodnight. He walked into the house as the lights of Candy's car faded down the street. The ocean washed the shore. The TV was on. His task force lay sprawled around the living room. Dell opened a beer.

Jim stood guard while Blue watched the news. Dell looked inside the refrigerator for another can of beer. He had nursed four beers that night, claiming sobriety. He commented on the wisdom of Richard Nixon. They discussed the war and the idea of détente. Could they be at peace with a Communist country?

"That noble experiment," a liberal had commented at the party in regard to the Soviet Union. "Bourgeoisie," said another. The well-to-do who attended the parties ranged from conservative to liberal. The conversation went back to Richard Nixon. They believed in détente. Dell sipped his beer. Jim surrendered his riot gun to Dell, telling him it had been a quiet evening. Dell stood guard.

All was silent. Blue went out to make his nightly rounds. Candy called at eleven. Jim accepted a beer and stood watch with Dell. They dozed. It was a peaceful night.

Blue came back. His watch was secure. They could sleep.

Jim had turned in. Dell stood guard.

Hank and Mabel were still in Fresno.

At six that morning, Dell started making coffee and smoked. Phil was his suspect in the murders, and Frank had agreed. Prostitution entered the case; they considered Good Look Salon as dealing in white slavery. Phil was not the good captain who steered a secure ship. He was involved in racketeering, Dell was sure.

Blue and Jim slept until ten. Dell made them eggs and toast and poured coffee for them.

Jim took Dell's riot gun. "I'll stand guard," he said.

Blue could find nothing of interest in the newspaper. Nixon had spent the weekend at Camp David. The war continued. There was stalemate in Indochina. Blue drank beer and read about the Utah Stars leading the American Basketball League and went back to sleep.

Jim listened to the radio. He liked rock music on the FM band. Noon came and passed. Jim and Dell spent the day quietly sipping brew and discussing the murder. Katie was dressed. It was three in the afternoon when Blue awoke.

Dell showered and shaved and got dressed. He was going to the Seaside Hotel and Bar on Highway 101 leading into Monterey. He got into his car and pulled out of the drive that curved in front of the house.

Jim and Blue watched TV. They had the whole evening to discuss Phil and the two killings as they played rummy and drank beer. They still had to keep so many people under observation. They were certain that a suave type was behind the homicide.

Dell was just after a couple of brews before going home for dinner. He pulled into the hotel, entered the bar, and ordered a beer. He smoked and drank until five, when he drove back to the house. It was still raining. Whitecaps formed on the ocean.

Blue served TV dinners after Dell returned. The three men drank beer and watched *Maverick* and then the news. They were all still concerned with the killings.

At eleven, Blue made his rounds, cruising the area around the magazine and driving by Mark's place. Blue came back and reported that it had been a quiet but rainy night.

Jim stayed up as Blue went to sleep. Jim smoked and thought about the case. He figured that Katie's killer had had a key to her apartment. It was April, and there had been no signs of the killer since the new year had begun. Jim drank coffee and smoked.

At nine, Dell was up, and Blue emerged in his impeccable sheriff's uniform. Dell poured coffee for the two and lit a cigarette. The three sat and smoked. They said little. Phil was in the crosshairs of the federal government.

There was going to be a party that evening at *Argo's*. Candy would be by at six to pick up Dell. They had no way of knowing that evening or the next morning why Heather didn't answer her phone. They found out the following morning.

PART THREE

MEMORIAL DAY

17

Heather was dead on the floor of her apartment. The time of her death was estimated to have been three in the morning. Blue had checked on Mark the night before so that ruled him out.

As had been the case with Katie, Heather was fully clothed. She lay stately in death. Heather had sunk to her knees with a rope twisted around her neck. The room was disordered, but there was no sign of blood. It appeared that she had not resisted her attacker.

Jim checked the doors and windows and found a patio door partly open. They dusted for shoeprints. Dell stood by, watching Blue take notes.

The trio could not explain Heather's death, but they knew it had occurred because the killer had penetrated their security apparatus.

"Relax on Mark," Dell said.

They all agreed. Mark had been at his home.

"A third murder," Blue said.

"Another murder and no apparent motive," Jim said.

Dell called Phil.

Phil took the news badly. "Continue your investigation," he told Dell.

Dell and Jim returned to their house, discussing the latest killing and the killer who had eluded them again.

Blue had made his rounds. The night was stormy. They were at a loss. Dell and Jim discussed the case. It had been Jim's responsibility to protect Heather. "What went wrong? I'm going to see Tory Anderson," said Dell.

Blue made sandwiches for lunch. They opened beers all around. Dell gave way to his emotions. "We have a third victim," he said. "Danielle was alone on a country road. What do we have here?"

Jim had no answer. He knew he had to report this to the Monterey police.

"Mark is not suspect," Blue said.

"Continue your patrol, Blue," Dell said.

The murder had occurred at three in the morning. They had been on guard. "She was awake and fully dressed," said Jim. "The killer broke in through the patio door."

"I don't agree," said Jim. "The front door was locked. The patio door was ajar. The killer left by the patio door."

"The party at *Argo's* let out at midnight," said Dell, "and the bars closed at two. I want us to talk to Tory."

Tory sat at the counter at Good Look Salon. Classes for the school's thirty girls went from eight to five. The top five models went to *Argo's* after they had earned their certificates in modeling.

"Was Danielle one of your models?" Dell asked Tory.

"Yes, she was."

"What do you do here?" Jim asked.

Tory was distraught. He had learned about Heather's death just that morning. Dell gave him a shot of whiskey.

"I'm the academy's supervisor."

Dell glanced at an album of graduates and noticed Katie's picture. The three left.

Back at the house, Jim began drinking. "What do you think of Tory?" he asked Dell.

"He's straight," Dell said.

"The murderer is a punk," Jim said.

Dell stood guard. He knew Jim was taking Heather's murder personally. All had been well at two the previous night when Blue had been on patrol.

Candy called and learned of Heather's death. Dell was relieved she was safe.

"We were home when she was killed," Dell said.

Jim sipped on a brew. Tory was under his protection. A killer had struck again. Dell did not know who it was, but he was narrowing it down. Mark was no longer under surveillance. The charges against him were not strong.

"Keep an eye on Candy," Dell told Jim. "We must protect her. Tory is also a suspect in all of this, but he could end up a victim, so protect Tory."

Jim and Blue drove to VIP's for coffee, which they though would do them good.

Jim mentioned that Jorgenson at narcotics thought the murder was drug related. "What do you think?" Jim asked Blue.

"I think it's the work of some young man," Blue said. "A rich punk."

"I agree," said Jim. "We're not far from an arrest."

They drank coffee in silence. The murder occupied their thoughts.

Jim left a tip as Blue paid the tab. They drove home.

Dell was standing guard and watching TV.

"Let's look into the East Commune," said Dell.

The three played cards as dusk fell. They were on watch.

The commune near Salinas filled their thoughts.

18

In Salt Lake City, Frank and Amanda waited to hear news of a stolen car ring in Fresno from Hank and Mabel. She told Frank that Dell had called. "Another murder, Frank."

"Tell Dell to cover all his bets," Frank said.

Amanda took notes as the two drank beer and smoked.

"They're searching for the killer," said Amanda. "Dell has a composite he's working on."

"Tell them to continue," Frank said.

They said little more as they drank and smoked. Frank left a tip and paid for the beer.

Amanda made a mental note to contact Mabel and Hank. She drove south on State Street and swung left on 33rd South.

It had been two weeks since Heather's death. Dell stood guard. He felt it was his fault as much as it was Blue's that Heather had died. "I was negligent, Jim," he said. "Keep an eye on Tory and that salon. Candy's at risk."

Dell handed Chico a pint of gin at a magazine party. "Compliments of the police," he said. He wanted information from Chico, especially about the East Commune.

"Thank you, Mr. Sandberg," Chico said.

Dell was certain that the killer was one of Phil's party guests. He drank beer while listening to the HoneyBees, who were well known in Monterey. Jonah Fitzgerald, the lead singer, could handle so many rock songs.

Cocaine, grass, and booze flowed freely at the event, but Dell took it in stride. He wanted to learn what he could about the East Commune.

Dell filled in Blue and Jim on the party when he got home that night, but he didn't have much to say.

Frank sat over another pitcher of beer. As a Mormon bishop, he preached on Sunday, but he was a US marshal the other days of the week. He was concerned about a car ring in Fresno and hoped Hank and Mabel could give him information about it.

Amanda came in and sat across from Frank, who poured her a beer. She mentioned that some of *Argo's* girls were Mormon, and the magazine could be charged with transporting girls across state lines, a federal offense.

Elder and Amanda considered Phil to be a well-connected racketeer, but Amanda mentioned that Dell didn't think so.

"What's Dell doing?" Frank asked.

Amanda couldn't answer that.

Dell sat down to write a fiction article he had entitled "The Assassin." It started, "Clad in dark trousers with a purple, pullover sweater and a nylon covering his face, he grasped a marine combat knife and killed. In Indochina? No, at home. He killed those who publicly dissented. He was an assassin." Dell described a home-front hero. Would Phil like it? It was a bit of Superman in modern times.

The war went on. Nixon had invaded Cambodia. The South Vietnamese had invaded Laos. A young South Vietnamese general had been killed. It was stalemate in Indochina in April 1971. Nixon was pulling the troops out based on his policy of Vietnamization, expecting the South Vietnamese to win their war. Nixon did not foresee defeat.

Dell kept a catalog of news clippings on the war. He had followed the newspapers since the beginning and had a good grasp of the conflict. Communism was at a stalemate in the bitter fighting. With this leitmotif, Dell wrote of a soldier who cruised the streets in the early hours of the morning and killed.

Dell knew that Mark was a Vietnam vet who had been in heavy fighting in '65. Was he their killer? Dell wanted to find out. His story would appear in *Argo's* July issue. It was late April, and he was a month ahead of his deadline with Phil.

Phil had taken the death of his paramour badly. Their liaison had not been well known at all. He sat at his desk and ate a cheese sandwich and sipped coffee. Heather and Good Look Salon had helped his magazine tremendously. She had also been one of his nonfiction editors. He was

ame**

72 ERIC PATRICK DANIELSON

convinced he was going to be the next victim. He picked up the phone and dialed Dell. He wanted protection.

Dell told Blue to include Phil on his surveillance rounds. They were looking for a veteran who masqueraded around Monterey.

Dell hoped Phil would like his fiction story, but he knew Phil was in a panic about the murders. His thoughts turned to Candy. She had told him she had an attack dog and lived with a group of girls in a house.

He walked through the rain to the bar on the beach, where Bobbie said hello and served him a beer. She knew he was a writer, and he knew she was divorced with a kid. Her old man had moved out, but she liked her job and her apartment.

After four beers, Dell left a tip and headed back.

It was five in the evening, and Blue was standing guard while Jim was drinking. Jim wanted details on Heather's death.

"Forensics should tell us," said Dell.

Jim was a hardened homicide detective. He told Dell they had all been murders.

"But drugs are involved," Dell said, and Jim agreed.

"The patio door was open, and it led to a garden," Jim said.

"It was three in the morning with nothing on the street," Dell said. "Check on it, Jim. Continue putting together what you can about Heather."

Blue, armed with the riot gun, sat in the living room, alert. He planned to head out later to check on Mark, who they had determined had been home on the morning of the murder.

"Who was the rock group at the party?" Jim asked.

"The HoneyBees," said Dell. "Their vocalist is a woman named Jonah."

He and Jim sat in the kitchen and discussed the triple killing over the phone with Hank and Mabel, who were still in Fresno checking on the car theft ring.

"What do you have?" Jim asked.

"A greeting card from a friend," said Dell.

They discussed all the people they were guarding, including Candy, but nothing seemed amiss that evening. They drank and watched TV.

Because Phil imagined himself a target of the assassin, Dell wanted Blue to include Burt in his surveillance.

Dell stood guard after Blue went to bed. He shaved and showered in the morning and put coffee on. Hank and Mabel were due from Fresno, and Jim was up. He relieved Dell as guard. Someone was always on duty, day and night. Dell went to bed. Jim and Blue played cards. They drank coffee. They talked. They had a profile.

Dell awoke at noon for lunch. Jim turned the riot gun over to Blue.

Phil sat in his restaurant, the White Glove, nursing a scotch and water while eating roast beef. He thought about how he always tried to be kind. He wondered how he had aroused such antipathy to his business enterprise. It wasn't a party night, so he drove home and was there by six. He thought of Danielle. She had been a prostitute at age nineteen. *How unkind*, he thought.

O n May 1, 1971, a Volkswagen came up the drive and stopped at the house. Mabel stepped into the house with Hank. She was laughing. Frank had made her a US deputy marshal. Amanda had called her in Fresno the day before.

Dell congratulated Mabel. "Welcome back," he told the disheveled travelers who had been gone a month.

"Are you ready for Monterey?" Dell asked Mabel.

"Yes," she replied.

"Keep cool for now," said Dell. "I want you to rest and let us see where we are. We have until Memorial Day. Did you know Heather was killed?"

"Heather at Good Look Salon?" Mabel asked.

"Yes," said Dell.

Mabel read Dell's "The Assassin" and gave it to Hank to read.

"Are you certain of the profile?" Mabel asked Dell.

"Yes," said Dell.

"Fiction," said Hank.

"Yes, fiction," said Dell, "but the profile is real."

The five cops started drinking the beer Mabel had brought.

"US deputy marshal," Dell said. "Frank told us how you had been instrumental to narcotics and vice in Salt Lake City. Congratulations on your promotion. You're a fed now."

"Blue and I congratulate you too," Jim said. "Good news."

Mabel left to buy more beer and TV dinners. Life would resume in the house.

After lunch, the five discussed the case. Hank and Mabel didn't talk much about their trip. "Amanda has our report," said Hank.

Mabel was silent. She trembled a bit as Dell and Hank pinned a deputy marshal badge on her blouse. Mabel took the oath. "I do solemnly swear to uphold the laws of the United States." They gave her two books as gifts, one by Margaret Mitchell and the other by Ayn Rand. She lit a cigarette. She gathered herself and emitted smoke. "Thank you all."

They drank beer, played cards, and discussed the case that was developing. They had a list of names of the West Coast underworld.

"Chico is a suspect," said Hank with a grin.

"A pint of gin," said Dell.

They were back in business in Monterey. Mabel smiled, drank beer, and smoked, while Hank drank as Blue and Jim dealt cards. They had their own perspectives. They discussed the killings and said they were sure Phil was somehow involved.

"What did Tory have to say?" Mabel asked.

"We didn't quite get down to nails with Tory," Dell said.

"We forget that Phil is the initial basis of our investigation," said Hank. They discussed Phil.

"I see no evidence of racketeering," Dell said.

"He uses his clout to get his way," said Hank, "but he's not a ruthless mobster."

"That he's a front for West Coast crime activity remains to be proven," Mabel said.

Jim and Blue represented local authority, while Dell, Hank, and Mabel were feds for this case, which crossed state lines.

"Phil's restaurant in Monterey is a hangout for mob figures," said Hank.

Blue nodded. He had the White Glove under surveillance.

"I think Phil's involved in prostitution and narcotics," said Mabel.

"We may prove racketeering," said Hank.

"Drugs are not too hard to prove with Chico," Mabel added.

They understood their case. It could include murder, but they needed evidence.

"We have a motive for murder in one or two arenas," Jim said.

"Candy speaks well of Phil," Dell said.

"Where did Heather fit into this?" Hank asked.

They sat and discussed so many questions. What emerged were some ideas as the five sought to solve the cases, but they were sure they were getting there.

They watched the news and then Alfred Hitchcock. Blue left on his patrol, while Jim stood guard. The rest went to bed.

Dell was up at six, drinking coffee and smoking. He relieved Jim. The morning passed. Mabel got up while Hank was in the shower. Blue got up. The gathered over coffee and discussed strategies for the remainder of the month. Hank and Mabel headed out, planning on returning that weekend. They wanted to scout Monterey.

Jim and Blue went to VIP's and watched people come and go. They discussed the killings and whether Phil was guilty of them.

"I think he is," said Blue. "Perhaps it surrounds him."

They were back at the house at three, and Jim stood guard.

21

Dell stood guard while Jim and Blue slept one morning in early May 1971. He put coffee on and smoked while waiting for his first cup. He thought of his profile. He had several suspects. He considered members of the underworld, who had a definite presence in Monterey. He thought of the year he had spent on the West Coast. Phil was suspected, but Dell thought he had been ruthlessly honest.

Dell had increased his vigilance since Heather's death. They tightened security around the many people involved. Danielle had been a hooker, but Katie had been a good girl and Heather an expensive mistress. There was so much to Phil. He spent the weekend in Sacramento. Hank and Mabel were on the road. The trail also led to Sacramento. There was San Francisco and Los Angeles. Was this indictment a reason of Phil?

Spring was in the air. A light breeze came off the Pacific. The temperature was warm. It was a lovely time to be in California. In Indochina, it was still a stalemate.

Dell, Blue, and Jim drank and talked about the case. Blue made sandwiches for the three.

Dell showered and lay down. There was a party that night at *Argo's*. Candy would be by to pick him up. She had given Phil her refusal on a future contract. Phil asked her to reconsider. Candy had told Phil she would reconsider, but she trembled.

"You don't have to pose," Dell had told her.

She didn't mind that. She was a monthly model.

Dell had admonished Candy. He was worried she would end up like the other girls.

Dell awoke at five and got ready. Blue took over guard duties. Jim had just turned on the TV. They had dinner.

Candy was at the door at six.

"Hello," said Dell.

"I'm just a little late," she said. It was ten after six.

Blue and Jim introduced themselves as Dell grabbed his coat.

Candy pulled out of the drive.

"Phil wants us to be more active socially," Candy said.

Dell had to agree. Candy mentioned Heather.

"Her death at Easter was not a coincidence," said Dell. "I want you to be careful."

At the party, Mark offered Dell a beer and mixed a daiquiri for Candy. The HoneyBees, a local sensation, were playing, and Jonah was singing.

"Can I buy you a drink?" Dell asked Jonah during one of her breaks. She accepted. The two talked.

Phil was seated, a tumbler of whiskey in hand. A dozen girls surrounded him. Candy was talking with Mark. Dell had told Mark that he and Chico were suspects.

Candy asked Mark if he had known Danielle, and Mark said he had.

Jonah excused herself. The HoneyBees were on.

"See you, Jonah," said Dell.

"It's all here at the party," Dell said to Candy.

"Is that so?" Candy said.

They sipped their drinks and mingled. The band struck up. Guests were dancing. Chico stood in a corner with his brown sack. Cigarette and marijuana smoke filled the air. Mark mixed cocktails and served sandwiches. There was vodka and caviar.

At ten, Candy wanted to leave, and Dell was home in half an hour.

Jim stood guard. Blue was about to assume his patrol. Dell relieved Jim with his riot gun. Jim retired while Dell sat up until six.

"You let me sleep," Jim said to Dell.

"Yes," said Dell.

They drank coffee. Jim smoked.

"Allow two friends to relieve you at guard," said Jim.

The three men ate breakfast. Candy was home safe. She had called the night before at eleven as instructed.

Dell lay down to sleep. Jim sat in the living room armchair with the riot gun. Should a hitman arrive, he was ready.

Dell awoke in the early evening. Jim was still on guard. Dell smiled.

"We let you sleep, deputy marshal. You had a good rest," Jim said.

Blue took over for Jim.

"I'll patrol at eleven," he said.

It was a tranquil May evening in Monterey. They watched the news and discussed the leads they were working on. Mark and Chico were suspects, but Jim had told them to consider a rich punk.

Dell drank beer and thought of the murders. He had allowed what had evolved to coincide with theory. He was sure they were looking for a paramilitary figure, not a Chico or a Mark. There had been a pack of cigarettes found on Danielle, but she had bummed smokes from the three sailors. Dell wondered about that and the facts of the other murders. *Who's the assassin?* he wondered.

Dell watched *I Spy,* a good show, and nursed a beer while Blue was on guard and Jim was playing solitaire. The murders, however, weren't far from their minds.

Blue prepared to go on patrol. He donned a light jacket. It was cool that evening. Dell assumed guard while Jim slept on the couch. Hank and Mabel were still on the road. Mabel had said she held a clue to Phil's activities.

Candy had called at eleven, and Blue was back by one. All was quiet in Monterey. Blue went to sleep after checking the doors and windows.

Dell thought of Heather's patio door and placed a bar at the base of theirs.

He thought of Jonah and the other girls who could end up the next victims.

22

Detective Pat Jorgenson, working narcotics with the Monterey police, went over the substance-abuse records of a number of homicide victims. The files were marked "US Marshal" but had local jurisdiction. Pat had prosecuted so many drug lords in the underworld, and there was evidence of narcotics use in the three murders. The feds didn't get involved in local and county matters. An underworld informer was suspected in this.

Pat organized an undercover team to investigate the homicides. A murder that crossed state lines was reason to involve the US marshals.

Dell represented the feds. He was a US deputy marshal who could look into underworld connections.

He was at home. Pat was at his desk as he surveyed local traffic. Pat looked at the street. He was familiar with a number of dealers and had them followed. He could report to Dell that things had been quiet for the last few months. He had compiled a list of everything they had on local drug traffic.

When drug dealing crossed state lines, Pat referred the matter to Dell, who was in touch with McDuff and Frank. Blue handled the red ball. Pat used his own personnel to infiltrate mob activity.

Blue was at home in the house. He had received a call from Pat and informed Dell that they were at an impasse in homicide and narcotics.

"Pat thinks it's the mob," Blue said.

"Yes," said Dell. *What was going on?* he wondered. Pat was standing by. He was a good cop. He handled grueling assignments in narcotics.

Dell showered and shaved. He was going bar hopping. Jim sat on the couch. He nursed a beer. Blue was jotting down notes.

Henry Weinhard's was seventy-five cents a glass at the place Dell visited. He ordered one and gave the bartender a dollar. He reviewed his police case and thought of the East Commune. He realized what had not been considered in this was Fort Ord, very near the commune.

Dell ordered another beer. He had the whole afternoon. It was a pleasant day in Monterey. There was a party the next night at Phil's. Dell sat and drank. He was home by five. Blue was standing guard. Dell opened a beer and sat. He was dealing with a federal case with local jurisdiction. He and Jim chatted. Homicide was the theme. They discussed the killings.

Blue stood guard. At eleven, he went on patrol. He was vigilant.

Nothing had been said of Mark or Chico since Heather's death. They suspected the drug underworld, dismissing Chico as a likely suspect. Dell had filed all this mentally. He wanted Blue to continue his night patrols. They were dealing with an assassin.

There was a beer in the refrigerator.

"It's coming," muttered Jim.

The clock struck six. The news came on. The war dragged on in Vietnam. The Pacific washed the shore by the house.

"I think Memorial Day," said Dell.

"Heather was killed at Easter. Katie died New Year's Day. Danielle died on the Fourth of July. Either Jonah or Candy is the target on Memorial Day."

Blue nodded in agreement.

"It's coming," Jim repeated.

Hank and Mabel had been scouting Monterey during May. They were undercover. Narcotics played a role in their disguise. Frank had employed them, as Dell knew.

Dell went to his meeting with Phil. He was at *Argo's* at ten. Phil welcomed him.

"What news?" Phil asked.

"I would like to know more of yourself and Heather," Dell said.

"Be discreet," said Phil.

The two were drawn into conversation. The morning passed.

Candy called. She would be by at six. The girl was all excitement. She obeyed Dell and called at eleven every night to let him know she was safe. She kept a loaded automatic in her nightstand. She knew Dell was after a night stalker in Monterey.

When Candy knocked at six, Dell was dressed in his jacket and ready to go.

He mentioned he had spoken with Phil that morning. Dell had learned that Heather had been Phil's mistress. He figured her death was aimed at the powerful man.

"What did Phil have to say?" Candy asked.

"He wishes to cooperate with the US marshals," Dell said. Dell was a treasury agent in Phil's mind.

Candy drove. She was not serious about Dell; she was strictly his escort at the parties. Dell remembered Katie. Dell had read the news. He was familiar with local narcotics investigations and in touch with the feds. He didn't think Candy did drugs. She just drank.

Phil welcomed them at the party. He was surrounded by beauty as usual. Mark handed Dell a Pabst and mixed a daiquiri for Candy. They saw Jonah with the band. Dell noticed Chico and Mark. He conversed with a few guests. Candy spoke with Phil, who was seated and sipping a drink. Dell noticed the drugs being used but remained silent about it.

Tory appeared, the first time since Heather's death. He scowled at Phil and said hello to Dell. Candy chatted with Mark. Chico stood in a corner with his paper sack. Marijuana smoke filled the air. Dell lit a cigarette. Tobacco fumes mingled with marijuana. The guests snorted cocaine. Dell nursed a beer.

"Have any ideas?" Tory asked Dell.

"Yes. We have a few clues. I suspect one or two people at the party."

"Can you make an arrest?" Tory asked.

"That's pending."

Tory moved away as the band struck up, Jonah singing. Candy joined Dell.

She dropped Dell off at ten. Blue was standing guard. Jim was sleeping. Blue went out on his patrol. Candy called. Dell assumed guard. Midnight struck in the house.

Dell rested. He had his riot gun.

The morning hours were quiet. Blue came in.

It was Friday morning.

At six, Dell made coffee. Blue was asleep, but Jim awoke.

"May I join you for coffee?" Jim asked.

Jim lit a cigarette. Smoke swirled as Dell and Jim discussed homicide. It was a local murder with interstate connections.

Frank called. He wanted an indictment.

"Yes, Frank," Dell said.

"It's your ball, Dell," Frank said.

Dell said good-bye. It was indeed his case. He was cautious of Phil. Frank had asked of Hank and Mabel. They would be home on the weekend. Frank had mentioned one word—skag.

23

Mabel's '58 Beetle pulled up in the drive. Hank and Mabel emerged, laughing. They had been to Sacramento, San Francisco, and Los Angeles and had spent the day in Monterey.

"We could have been back last night but decided to stay in a hotel. Let us tell you what we know," Mabel said.

"Good," said Dell. "We'll talk after lunch."

Mabel had bought TV dinners, which she put into the oven. They ate lunch. Jim and Hank exchanged glances. They discussed the case. They were looking for a solitary figure in Monterey or close by. The killer was a paramilitary.

They discussed Phil, heavily involved in the porn business. And his restaurant was suspected of being a front for mob activity. That could warrant an indictment.

"We had dinner at the White Glove last evening," Mabel said. "It's a respectable place."

Dell accepted this argument in defense of Phil.

They had grounds for an indictment.

"Who do you suspect in Phil's organization?" Mabel asked.

"There are a hundred guests at the party, but we're looking at Mark and Chico and Tory and the *Argo's* staff," said Dell. "We're looking for a paramilitary figure."

Jim still thought they should look for a punk.

"Why don't we prosecute this? Why don't we indict Phil?" Jim asked.

They were all agreed, except for Dell.

"Welcome back from your trip," said Dell.

"What did you find?" Blue asked.

"We found Phil's business office and bank account in Reno," Hank said.

"The East Commune and maybe nearby Fort Ord also figure in this," Dell said.

"Let us see what Army CID can put together in this," said Dell.

It was the middle of the month. They awaited Memorial Day. It was a bright and sunny day in Monterey. They drank beer and played cards.

Marshal McDuff stood in the doorway. "What do you have?" he asked.

"We have skag as central to the case," said Dell.

McDuff looked at the five.

"They smoke skag at the East Commune," added Dell.

"I have authority to prosecute this case," said McDuff.

Dell stood at attention. "Yes sir."

Dell still wondered about Fort Ord.

Evening came. Mabel cooked dinner. Blue and Jim stood guard. Dell made coffee, and Mabel came from her room for some. She lit a cigarette and talked with McDuff.

McDuff accepted a cup of coffee. He mentioned skag. Dell had been well informed. "Phil is a powerful man. He's implicated in murder, but we have a question of jurisdiction," McDuff said.

Blue, Jim, and Hank joined them.

"Everyone's present," McDuff said. "The case is a federal case."

McDuff poured another cup of coffee.

When Candy came at six, Dell introduced her to McDuff.

Dell was dressed for another *Argo's* party. He and Candy left.

They all knew matters were coming to a head. Memorial Day drew near.

"What are your findings?" Phil asked Dell.

Chico stood by with his brown paper bag full of substance abuse. Dell looked in his direction. Heroin had never been mentioned.

Mark handed him a Pabst and Candy a daiquiri.

"Hello Jonah," said Dell when she walked up.

"Hello Dell. What do you think?"

"Be careful," Dell said.

"Yes sir," Jonah said.

They discussed the case. Phil was an iconoclast who happened to be in good standing nonetheless, it seemed to Dell.

"Good luck," said Dell as Jonah headed for the band. Dell returned to Candy.

Phil sat in a chair on a raised platform. A dozen beauties surrounded him; they were wearing swimsuits and striking provocative poses.

Tory arrived, and Mark mixed him a drink. Chico conducted business in full view of Dell. The guests discussed the nonfiction that appeared in *Argo's*. Dell took all this in.

At ten, he and Candy left. They had been there since seven and had mingled. "I'll give you a call by eleven," said Candy as Dell got out of the car. The breeze off the ocean was mild.

Blue was on guard. He would patrol at eleven. McDuff, Jim, Hank, and Mabel were watching TV and drinking beer.

Blue was home by one. Hank and Mabel were on guard. She had her loaded service revolver with her.

The others in the household were asleep.

Dell slept. Mabel planned to wake him at six.

Night time passed in the house.

Mabel drank coffee and smoked Salems on that musty May night as Blue slept.

When Dell got up, he told Mabel to go to sleep. Mabel holstered her revolver and went to her room to sleep. He sat in the living room, his riot gun leaning against the wall.

The household was awake by ten. McDuff stood guard, and Dell went out. Mabel made breakfast as Blue drank coffee and smoked.

Dell came back at two, but he left again at five. McDuff was quiet.

Blue went out on patrol at eleven and was back by one.

Mabel was on guard again. Dell relieved her at guard. Candy had called.

The night passed. The clock chimed six.

Dell put a pot of coffee on and lit a cigarette. He had finished a pack during the night.

Mabel and Dell drank coffee and smoked. She gave him her views on the cases and told him of the leads she and Hank were following. Dell told her he thought Phil had finesse but was not dishonest.

Dell went out at twelve and was home by three. He saw Blue reading his notebook and McDuff drinking beer. They turned on the TV and learned that Phil had been indicted on federal charges.

In the evening, they drank and played chess and card games. They discussed Seaside, Monterey, and the California spring.

Dell stood guard and smoked. Wednesday night passed, and the household awoke for Dell's coffee. Dell went to sleep. Candy was coming by at six that evening. McDuff was silent, but they were all waiting for something to happen.

At noon, Jim went out. Blue talked to Pat on the phone about the cases and narcotics.

At six, Candy picked up Dell, and they went to a magazine party. Phil was pleased with Dell's writing, for which he was getting praise. Phil asked Dell where he was in the murder cases, thinking Dell could give him a clue.

Dell stood with Candy. They discussed Vietnam with other guests.

At ten, they drove home. Candy kissed Dell goodnight and promised to call at eleven.

"It will be tonight. Candy is home alone," Dell said.

McDuff gave his orders. A squad car stood by outside. Hank, Mabel, Blue, and Jim were up. Dell got in the squad car. The group drove to the White Glove. It was on that place that the case had focused. It was midnight.

PART FOUR

SEASIDE

25

It was June 1971. Dell sat in his room at a roadside hotel near Seaside. Hank and Mabel had returned to Fresno for the month. Blue had returned to regular duty cruising the county. Jim had returned to his desk at homicide. Local jurisdiction was assisting a federal case. McDuff had gone home to Stockton.

Dell opened a beer. It was a warm summer. He was clad in shorts. It was a few minutes after noon. He was on call to California. He reported to Frank in Utah and was liaison to McDuff. In cooperation, they had an outline of an investigation.

They had predicted a homicide on Memorial Day, but the killer had not struck. That July would mark the one-year anniversary of Danielle's death. Jim was a shrewd detective. He had a degree in police science, and he was sure they were dealing with a punk, while Dell thought they should be looking for a paramilitary figure. Dell finished his beer and thought about Chico and Mark. But he was looking for a third suspect.

At two, he showered and dressed in slacks and a summer shirt and went to the hotel bar, where the bartender knew him.

"A Henry's on tap," said Dell.

He sat at the bar and smoked in the quiet bar. A few people entered. A few people left. The afternoon passed. Dell smoked. At five, after five beers, he had a bite to eat at the bar. He went to his room to rest. He was groggy from the beer. He slept.

At midnight, he woke up and headed to the hotel's all-night restaurant. Back in his room, he retrieved a beer from the cooler he had in his room. He lit a cigarette. A sheaf of typed papers lay on the desk. He was compiling a collection of articles. He glanced at his notes. He was an expert on Indochina, it was said. He wanted to turn his articles into a book.

The next day, he talked with McDuff, who stopped by with some instructions on the investigation. "We need to look at the commune. We need to penetrate the obvious and figure out what undercurrents there are," McDuff said. "Our suspect attends the parties or is subsurface to the parties." McDuff left. He was on his way to San Francisco to talk with a narcotics officer.

Dell was up the following morning at seven. He took a shower, dressed, and popped the top on a beer. He opened the patio door of his room on the pleasant morning. The beach was only a few yards away. He sat in a patio chair and drank his beer. He thought of what McDuff had to say to him the day before. "We're looking at a third suspect. It can be proven that Chico and Mark were not involved in one or two of the killings," McDuff had said. "Possibly, there's more to Phil than we've thought."

"Phil knows or is a victim himself of our suspect," Dell had said.

"The entire purpose of your attending the parties is to become acquainted with *Argo's*," McDuff had said. "It's to get to know the people and the surroundings. Our suspect is inarticulate, so keep attending the parties," McDuff had told him.

Dell finished his beer and went back into his room. Two hours later, he was dressed in slacks, shirt, and shoes and was heading for the restaurant bar. He sat down and lit a cigarette. The bartender brought him a beer.

"How are you, Sandberg?" the bartender asked. He replaced the ashtray.

"Very good," said Dell. "But we still have several profiles to establish."

"Dell, I believe you're on target," the bartender said.

Dell drank several beers before leaving the bar and walking on the shore for a while. Back in his room, he sat at his desk and smoked. With McDuff's authorization, he would continue his investigation. He meant to visit the commune and keep on attending Phil's parties. He was on the hunt for the murderer. He penned a letter to Mabel and Hank and posted it at the front desk.

The opium at *Argo's* was mixed in with the murders. Jim had a composite of their suspect. Jim mentioned that seltzer water, not opium or skag, was the beverage employed. The murders all involved *Argo's*. Mark might know what Jim meant.

A hot roast beef sandwich with coffee was on his mind as he walked to the restaurant. He had another coffee. It was seven in the evening on a June night. He left a tip, paid his bill, and returned to his room for some sixteen-ounce Buds in is cooler and more smokes. He drank five beers and smoked half a pack of cigarettes before he fell asleep in his clothes.

At five, he rose to shower and shave. He combed his hair and brushed his teeth. He donned a light sports jacket. He stepped out of his room into the hall of the hotel. He walked through the lobby and went to the parking lot. He drove a '70 Super Sport.

He got into his car and pulled out of the lot. He headed north on Highway 101.

As a US marshal, McDuff's jurisdiction covered central and eastern California from his home in Stockton. He wore a slouch hat and gun belt and had a Winchester in his pickup. He represented federal law enforcement in the Sacramento River Valley, on the western slope of the Sierra Nevadas. McDuff avidly patrolled the region, apprehended evildoers, and brought them to justice. He had shot it out with dope smugglers and car thieves all the way to the Nevada border. He was tall, strong, and upright. He had a full moustache. He knew every hoodlum and con in eastern California.

His investigations into interstate trafficking and pornography carried him to Monterey, Phil's territory. He was after racketeers and drug smugglers who abounded in the area. Monterey, a small coastal city with a good harbor, attracted foreign elements from northern Mexico and abroad, including those who supplied Chico and other local dealers. For this reason, McDuff was interested in *Argo's*, even though he thought it was a legit magazine. He realized there was an impasse in the investigation of the triple homicide even though they suspected Mark and Chico. He knew there was a killer at *Argo's*. McDuff pulled at his moustache. An air of suspicion fell on Phil's entire enterprise.

Dell conc???ed something suspect that was not yet perceived. McDuff fron???ed. US Deputy Marshal ???ndberg was not sympathetic to indictment. He could ascertain that the charges filed did not have argument. That murder fell on *Argo's* magazine following federal district court proceedings is what Sandberg and McDuff himself could reason. Monterey homicide had a profile of yet another suspect.

McDuff chewed tobacco. He knew that modern sophisticates abhorred those who chew tobacco, but he had found that chewing helped him concentrate. It was a local killing but crossed state lines. McDuff was interested. He spat. At home in Stockton, he sat at his desk. He had a mug of coffee. He monitored police traffic with his two-way radio. A rifle rack adorned the wall of his study.

He employed Hank and Mabel as undercover police in Fresno, the basis of their investigation at South Tahoe. There were a few leads and facts to establish their investigation. Dell had a free hand, assisted by Monterey homicide and the county sheriff. And Dell stayed in touch with Frank in Salt Lake City.

McDuff made a salad and fried some ham and potatoes for dinner. He generally drank coffee. He had a beer once a week or so, but nothing harder.

He washed his supper dishes and sat down with a cup of coffee. He thought of the murders. Phil was a pawn in a high-stakes situation. There were several winds blowing in separate directions. McDuff was sure that the murders were some sort of power play within *Argo's*. McDuff went to sleep at ten and got up at four, as was his habit.

Hank and Mabel reported to him. He called them Swanson and Martinez. They were effective in bringing to light several facts in the case.

McDuff made breakfast. It was the weekend in Stockton. He decided to relax. As sheriff, he was on duty seven days a week, but he made it a point of relaxing as much as he could on weekends. He took care of some gardening and went shopping, getting back by one. He spent the rest of the day listening to his police radio and drinking coffee. He planned to go the next day to Imperial Valley to meet Hank and Mabel. He also planned to see Dell in a matter of days.

He read a letter from Galbraith, a deputy marshal in San Francisco. After keeping tabs on the comings and goings at the magazine, Galbraith thought that the magazine was not directly involved.

He drove to Silver City and had lunch with Hank and Mabel, who were hitchhiking to San Francisco.

"Please proceed," he told Hank and Mabel.

He returned to Stockton at six that evening. His thoughts were on Sandberg. It was Dell whom he thought had the best take on the murders. He would go with Dell.

Mark was a murder suspect. He had learned this from Dell at an *Argo's* party. He had thought Dell was just a writer, but Dell had told him he was a deputy marshal. Suspicion hung heavily in the air, but Mark kept on serving drinks. He knew Chico was under suspicion as well, but neither showed any emotion.

Phil continued to preside at his parties with little said. They all felt vulnerable. No one was safe. It had been quite a year. Mark had guessed that the killer had been a regular attendee at the parties. He thought the murders were internal, not external.

Mark knew that Dell was aware of the drugs being used at the parties. He could tell Phil that Heather's death was a finish to the business entity. Internal or external was the question. Dell also thought this. This is what brought him to the parties. In one year, he had become as familiar with the guests as was Mark.

One evening, Dell mentioned to Mark that the murders could be external. His May article in *Argo's* had made him a guest at the party. In it, he looked at both sides of the war, pro and con, with a great deal of reflection.

Mark served sandwiches and mixed drinks. He had known Burt for several years. He also knew Tory. He had known Heather. Burt had given him a job at *Argo's* as an editor.

As Dell sipped a brew, he could say in light of observation that the murders were external, but that didn't make things any easier.

Phil left at eleven, though the party continued until midnight, when Mark went home. His business expense account let him rent the Jaguar he drove. He served as a financial executive advisor to Phil. He had a degree from Southern Cal and was clean cut and clean shaven. He lived alone and ran a catering service that supplied the sandwiches, caviar, and booze at the parties.

He fixed himself an egg nog with rum and fell asleep, but he was up at six and ready for work at eight at *Argo's*. In the afternoon, he took care of his catering service; he catered events at many area businesses. But then he was back at *Argo's* at six to tend bar. Icing down the champagne, vodka, and beer took but a moment.

At seven fifteen, Phil arrived, and the party was underway, complete with live music. Mark was busy mixing drinks and emptying ash trays. He had been at his post for several years and knew most of the guests, conservatives and liberals alike. *Argo's* offered debate, not a slanted view of happenings either by the right or left tabloids. Phil waved a wand when it came to the prose he published. The highlight of the magazine was its girls, but since Heather had died, that part of the magazine was in jeopardy.

He saw Dell. "Hello sir," he said. He had beer chilled for Dell.

"Good evening, Mark," Dell said cordially.

Mark asked Dell about his recent article. "Do you really think that détente is viable in the Cold War?" Mark asked.

"I believe we're in a strong position," said Dell.

"Enjoy yourself, sir," Mark said.

Dell mingled with familiar faces, but he didn't speak much of the murders; he still had suspects, however. He left at ten. Phil left at eleven. Mark wrapped up at midnight. The suite closed. Mark drove home. He rarely went out after the parties.

Dell had a car, a hotel room, and an expense account. He was busy, and he felt the tension at *Argo's*, but he liked Phil, who seemed to be holding up. Phil trusted Dell.

"Cheer up, Mark," Phil said to Mark.

"There is a clue in your direction."

Mark smiled. He was free under his own volition. He would not give in. He would do as Burt did. They would not self-aggrandize at *Argo's*. They meant to apprehend the killer.

Mark edited a feature in the morning, while he and his staff of six worked the catering business that afternoon. Businesses and organizations in Monterey liked his banquets and the music he arranged for.

He realized that by then, Dell had learned all about the magazine and knew Monterey. Mark no longer felt he was a suspect. He trusted that Dell would find the murderer.

28

Jonah was a successful singer and keyboard player in several groups. Her vocals were lovely, as was she. She was well known and well respected in the local music scene as a performer and backup vocalist. She played clubs in Monterey, Carmel, and Seaside.

Mark had arranged for her to play the parties at *Argo's*, and she and the HoneyBees enlivened the place, even though the parties there bored her. She'd be home at eleven on those nights. She'd have a glass of sherry, unwind, and check her door before going to sleep. She was fully aware of the trauma the murders had inflicted on *Argo's* staff. The bogeyman stalked. She kept a loaded revolver in her nightstand.

All the other women involved with *Argo's* were worried as well; they were waiting for the killer to strike again, but they were hoping the police would find him before he did.

Jonah was up at six. Her condo was in Seaside, so she could walk along the shore. The magazine occupied her thoughts. She knew several fashion models there, and she appreciated the fact that Phil liked her.

She was busy on weekends with gigs and her volunteer work for non-profits in the area, but she spent many hours at *Argo's* parties and had gotten to know Dell, who had told her he was a narcotics cop who seemed to ignore the drugs at the parties. She was happy to know a cop.

Her encore at the magazine parties was always the same. The HoneyBees accompanied her. The guests liked her solos. But she enjoyed her peaceful nights with a glass or two of sherry, nothing stronger—no booze or drugs. She felt secure in her condo, but she had known Danielle and the other victims.

She did her best at the parties to entertain the guests, even though the tension the murders had produced was palpable. Everyone thought it was just a matter of time until the murderer would claim another victim.

The smoke-filled parties continued, but she'd always leave in her Datsun at ten and be safe in her condo by eleven.

She had come from Elko, Nevada, ten years earlier, with her guitar and her vocal abilities. She was a churchgoer who believed in the Bible and Greek philosophy. She had mentioned to Dell that she liked Aristophanes, and he had told her he liked her music.

Dell warned Jonah, "A playboy type is working around here."

Jonah thought of the West Coast and California. At the beginning of the century, it had been the Bay Area and the Barbary Coast.

She mentioned this to Dell.

"Do you think Barbary?" she asked Dell.

"I think a smiling type and some seclusion."

Frank sat alone at the bar and grill on 21st South with a pitcher of beer. He had come from humble origins. His father had raised his son strictly. Frank had attended a Bible college in Cedar City, Utah, for two years and had left college armed with a Bible and an understanding of the Book of Mormon.

He went to Salt Lake City and enrolled in the LDS Church. He became a deputy marshal, and the years went by. At age fifty-eight, he was US marshal in a district in Utah. He was also bailiff in a federal court and had a desk at the courthouse in Salt Lake City.

He had established the bar and grill as the place where he met Salt Lake City police. He was there daily at noon and at three, and he would drink and smoke, his only two vices.

"Another pitcher of beer," Frank said to a waitress.

He had just sat with a couple from Phoenix who were pursuing an investigation in Scottsdale. Elder knew the authorities in Phoenix.

A young man sat at Frank's booth. He had long hair. Elder poured him some beer. "Relax, son. I don't arrest long hair. It's just a style. You reported something in Toole County that harmed you and your girl. There's a federal reservation in Toole. It connects."

Frank smoked. He was a large man with heavy hands. He stood six feet tall.

"I will pursue this for you," he told the young man. "Rest your mind a bit."

The young man thanked him and left.

Frank drank and smoked. He had McDuff's report from Stockton. He thought of his deputy in Monterey pursuing something that defied indictment.

A couple sat down, and Frank introduced himself.

"I'm a federal marshal. What can I do for you?"

The couple explained that they were from another state and had had a problem that had followed them from there.

"I'll see what I can do," Frank said.

Business was done. He finished the pitcher of beer. He was ready to go. He got up to leave the bar and grill, to which he brought a lot of business.

Frank drove to his home in Magna, at the foot of the Oker Mountains. He met his wife at six. She was a virtuous Mormon woman. They had two teenage sons. They were a solid, middle-class family.

Frank felt that communism threatened the world. The Soviets represented an enemy of the West, but the conflict in Indochina had arrested the spread of communism. Elder sat back after dinner at his desk.

He generally slept fitfully for only a few hours every night. He would rise at four and get to the courthouse at six. He would drive to Toole and Orem, nearby counties, but be back at the bar and grill at noon and then at the courthouse by one.

At the courthouse, the district attorney accosted him.

"Frank. Have you served a summons in Monterey?"

"No. That's been deferred," said Frank. "We're investigated the allegations, but they seem to be weak."

The district attorney frowned. "You consider so many charges as simply allegations?"

"Yes," said Frank. "I want Dell to investigate them thoroughly."

"You may disprove them," said the DA.

Frank deferred to the DA.

At three, he left for his bar and grill. He had checked into the stories of the people he had talked to that morning. At four, he was back at court, where he worked until six. But many days, he worked later than that.

The next day, he left for the courthouse early and was there at six. He worked until noon on several investigations. His agenda was full, and he employed a number of personnel. He was an LDS bishop as well, and he was active in his church and community as a fed and a minster.

Chico had no idea how to defend himself against suspicion of murder. He had told his old lady, Maria, that the law suspected him of peddling dope, but he had no idea why Dell suspected him, or Mark, for that matter, of murder. He decided to keep a low profile as he dealt dope. He was making good money, and he planned on retiring soon. That is, if he stayed alive. He wondered why Dell overlooked his dealing at the parties. He guessed it was because Dell was more interested in the murders. He knew Dell was an astute cop. Chico was pretty sure Dell had left him alone with his drug trade because it was all conducted in state. Only if he crossed state lines would it become a federal matter. So Chico would deal at the parties and simply observe Dell, the fed and the writer.

Even though Dell suspected him, he kept to his schedule of driving the kids to school and then selling drugs during the day. He had his own idea of who the killer was, and he knew he could handle the killer with his stiletto.

Chico thought about when the killings had begun. He knew most of the guests and figured it was an outside job, but he didn't tell anyone of his suspicions. He just dealt drugs at the parties and elsewhere.

He had been born in El Paso. He was a US citizen by birth who had found his way to California as a dope peddler. All was going well at *Argo's* parties, at which Chico was a regular. One evening, Chico asked Dell, "Hello, sir. How do you do?"

Dell said he was doing well.

It was July 1971. Summer was at its height. Chico kept peddling drugs across Monterey County and making good money. It had been a year since

Danielle's body had been found, and he knew the cops were continuing their investigation that had extended to Ford Ord.

He made a bank deposit before making it home with his pint of gin. He spent an hour cooling down. He risked arrest and possession. He had traded for years without a conviction. He confounded the cops. He made good money. It was only in the wee hours of the morning that he could sleep. He wanted to figure out who the murderer was and who was menacing Phil. So he kept quiet and did his business, keeping his thoughts and his conclusions to himself, but he talked to people in Salinas, near where Danielle had been killed.

In the meantime, he dealt drugs and drank his gin after hours.

He was always welcome at the magazine parties. "Hey Chico," many would say when they saw him. He was always friendly with his customers, but he knew the feds weren't to be taken lightly, and he wondered what they knew. The feds were the hardest people in the world to figure out, but he took their concerns seriously.

31

Tory Anderson had had a well-established routine at the salon until Heather had been murdered. Models had been scared off by her murder, but Tory was still trying to run a school in spite of Heather's loss, which he felt keenly. A few girls conquered their fears and continued attending the school.

He attended the parties at *Argo's* at night and took an interest in news and information about the murders after working the day at the salon.

"We're keeping the school going," he'd told Phil, who applauded Tory's determination.

Argo's magazine continued to function as well. There were monthly issues to produce in spite of the murders.

Tory read a lot, mostly fiction but also biography and history. He took an interest in Far East history. He'd always get up at five and be at work at seven. He liked Monterey, but the police were questioning him closely about Heather's death. He had told the police what he had known. He had said goodnight to her the night of her death and had learned about it only the next morning.

Tory was convinced that the murders were meant to bring down Phil. Tory stood by Phil, whom Tory considered a scrupulous person, as Tory had told the police. He had said that Phil was a tough businessman but put out a good magazine with articles and photos. Tory stood by Phil.

Off hours, when Tory wasn't reading, he was playing pool and relaxing at the bar he had at his place. He'd entertain guests and serve them cocktails. He maintained cordial relations with many people, including those he met at the parties.

He had been a dogface in World War II who had also served in Korea and had gone on to college. He ran the salon, which was in a Spanish-style building in Monterey, and he visited the White Glove restaurant frequently.

But Tory was cautious. He kept a loaded rifle at home. He would not be caught by an assassin. He was determined to keep the school going with imagination and hard work in spite of Heather's death.

Tory was an aggressive person who paid attention to details at school and elsewhere. He had a degree in business and knew accounting. He wasn't married, so he was devoted to his work.

At one magazine party, he was drinking whiskey and soda and talking with Phil as the two looked over the crowd. Tory talked about the school, and Phil mentioned that things were going well at the magazine.

"We're rising to the occasion," Phil said.

Tory left at nine. He finished the evening with a nightcap. He retired at eleven.

The following evening, he was entertaining a psychologist and a journalist from Berkeley in his apartment. Tory asked them, "Tell me about serial killers." The three discussed the murders, and the psychologist talked about the serial killers he had studied.

Several weeks later, Tory was invited to a luncheon at the White Glove. Phil presided over the event in a full business suit. It was August, and the events of the year were just memories. Tory's work went on. He was adamant that the school would continue. He thought of Blue, the sheriff, who had spoken to him about Heather's murder.

Tory's thoughts went deeper than anyone could fathom.

32

Phil was home from work. He wasn't hosting a party that night. He drank cognac and thought about his publishing empire and his other businesses, and he worried about the possibility of federal indictments.

Phil had few vices. He smoked and drank and had some girlfriends, but he was in essence a modest man, and he owed nobody anything. He was a fair and tolerant boss to his employees and also his writers. Good writers were hard to come by. He had at most a dozen writers on whom he could count.

He finished his cognac in his small ranch house in Monterey. He spent the evening at his desk in his home office watching TV. He slept soundly, got up early, and was at work by eight. He was forty. He'd been married twice and had children, but at the time, he was alone.

He was afraid that *Argo's* had become a target of the murderer because it published articles that dissented with the war in Vietnam, but he wasn't sure Dell believed that.

Phil had a degree in English, which had drawn him into the publishing business. He had an eye for good photography as well as good writing. He approved of what was imaginative and provocative, but an undercurrent of fact underlay his magazine. He liked Dell's writing because it was based on facts in spite of Dell's conservative bent. Dell seemed unconcerned with the drug dealing and the prostitution at his parties; he seemed more concerned with the murders, and Phil respected Dell's professionalism. But Phil wondered whether Dell would indeed prosecute him.

He went to work the next morning to check the proofs of the latest issue. His circulation was a half million copies monthly, but some of his competitors disputed this figure. Phil figured that was just professional jealousy.

He was home after five that afternoon, again drinking cognac and reading the paper. He thought of the murders of Danielle, Katie, and Heather. He thought of the investigation. He hoped Dell would bring his investigation to a conclusion and indict a killer.

He was foremost a businessman with a number of interests, including the White Glove restaurant, one of his flagship enterprises that employed a good number of people and was popular in Monterey. But he enjoyed his solitude.

He had talked with Dell about another article, one that would stimulate debate in his magazine, which served as his alter ego. He enjoyed another cognac. He was in suspense about the investigation, but he had good nerves. He could see this through.

PART FIVE

THE WHITE GLOVE

33

In September 1971, Dell was in his hotel suite in Seaside, on the shore and west of Carmel. He drank a beer and made a meal of eggs and bacon he kept in the refrigerator and prepared in the small kitchen in his suite.

He got to work on an article for *Argo's*. He could see the beach just outside. The US marshal's department had paid for the suite for a month as Dell worked on the case. Phil seemed to be the target of the killer's intentions; Phil's magazine was provocative.

Phil drank beer, which was ambrosia to him. He wrote of Thieu and Ky and Diem, who had stood against Ho Chi Minh. Between drinking beer, he drank coffee. He thought he should drink more coffee. He had until New Year's, Frank had told him, to find the killer.

Dell knew that Mark thought it was someone outside of the magazine, outside of the parties. He thought Chico and Phil were innocent.

Dell had been to the commune a number of times and had spoken with the leader and Danielle's boyfriend. The people there raised vegetables and rabbits amid enjoying music and art. It was a friendly gathering of mostly college-age people.

Dell drank a second beer. An internal or external murderer? A third figure suggested itself. He thought of his past in Korea and in Salt Lake City. He had attended college and had dated a number of women. He had had one or two flames but was not in a relationship. He was content at age forty. He was a US marshal and a journalist who also wrote fiction. His typewriter was the catalyst in the police case.

He meant to finger the murderer for the sake of his victims' survivors.

He smoked, but he didn't chain smoke. He drank. He didn't consider himself a health advocate. Healthy people had health problems. He finished a beer and grabbed his jacket. He carried an automatic in his waistband. He was on his way to bar hop and talk to people. That's where he hoped to find someone irrational enough to target the girls and the magazine. That was why he patronized bars.

He drove downtown to a quiet bar and ordered a beer. Few people came and went. The drinkers there were intent on their cocktails.

An hour later, he headed to a similar bar. A woman entered as two men left. Dell ordered her a drink. They talked, but he wasn't interested, and she left. He ordered another beer and watched the news about Indochina.

Back at his hotel, he rested for an hour before he stepped outside on his patio and smoked and watched the surf hit the shore. He went back inside, opened a beer, and stared at the typed pages on his desk. He thought of his case. His killer. His fiction.

He would continue his case until Christmas. Frank was getting impatient, but Dell would provide a few facts. There was no organized, systematic wrongdoing at *Argo's*.

Dell enjoyed the evening. He drank a fresh brew. On his desk was another typed page that dealt with the clash between East and West. Vietnam was a theater in the proletarian struggle. Dell was middle class.

He slept and woke at eleven that evening. He turned on his desk lamp, showered, and changed. He fried some bacon, drank a beer, and smoked. He wrote more about the Thieu government and the Vietnamization of the war.

At four in the morning, he went down to the restaurant for coffee. He was a welcome guest. The bartender thought Dell was a house detective.

At seven that morning, he took a seat on the patio. At eight, he had breakfast. At ten, he went to the bar and had a few beers until he ate lunch.

He went back to his room and lay down. He wrote about Vietnam and thought about the murders. He imagined a person, a partygoer. He thought of Chico, Phil, and Tory. Jim still thought they should be looking for a punk. That was something to go on.

Dell got up at four, showered, shaved, and dressed in slacks, shirt, and jacket. He carried an 8 mm Browning automatic. He slipped a pen knife and his room key in his pocket.

McDuff would see him in a week, and he had much to say to McDuff. The US marshal had stood by him.

At five, Dell lit up and opened a beer and sat on the patio. Evening came. There was still a war in Indochina. He sat back to think.

34

Candy felt safe with her housemates and Champion, her German shepherd, and Blue had told her the police were on guard for the murderer who roamed Seaside and Carmel. She had escorted Dell to the parties frequently and knew he was on the track of the murderer. She trusted Dell.

She had been the portrait of the month in *Argo's* after getting her certificate from the salon. She had kept a low profile in September, but Phil wanted her to attend his parties. He had hired her for an executive position as well as for modeling. She worked business hours and proofread much of the journalism that went into the magazine. She liked Monterey, where she had moved after graduating with a business degree from the University of Virginia with honors.

On weekends, she would drive her Karmann Ghia around the Monterey area when she didn't walk. She was not disturbed.

She considered Dell a lonesome cowboy, a soft-spoken federal agent. "We'll catch the killer," Dell had told her. She believed him and felt protected. But a killer still was on the loose.

She sat at breakfast in her room and relaxed. She drank tea and read the paper. She planned on going out at ten to shop in Monterey. She wanted to relax from the hectic magazine schedule during the week, when she was always facing deadlines.

She left the house and returned several hours later. She ate a sandwich and had coffee. She picked up a book. She always enjoyed a good novel. Some of the other girls in the house cooked supper that Saturday evening, then they watched TV.

Early next morning, she went to church. She was a devout Christian.

She had had religious doubts at one time and had disavowed God, but later, she had come back to God. On Sunday afternoon, she relaxed. She read the paper. She neither smoked nor drank spirits, but she allowed herself some wine every once in a while.

The next morning, she was at work early, at six. Phil was there, and others arrived at seven or so. She proofed the articles for the next issue under Phil's supervision.

She was home late that afternoon and had dinner, a cold plate her housemates had set aside for her. She drank some Chablis and read the paper.

Her routine was the same the next day.

She was twenty-seven and was enjoying the West Coast. She thought of the impasse in the Vietnam War. She had mixed feelings about the war. She thought preserving South Vietnam was a worthy goal. She knew all about Korea.

Phil gave her some compliments on her work just before she left for the day. Champion met her at the door; he pawed her, and she petted him.

Several girls cooked dinner, and she read until eight.

She thought of the magazine and the murders, but she trusted the police and refused to be intimidated anymore. She was sure they would find the murderer.

Blue was in his patrol car, scouting his county. He stopped at a rock quarry in east Monterey County at noon. He ate a sack lunch and drank some bottled water. He drove back to Monterey. He wanted to talk to people.

He knew many people by sight and would ask those he didn't know, "What's your business here?" He had been sheriff for twelve years and was well liked. He had solved a number of murders. He figured it was a solitary figure they were looking for. He thought drugs could be involved.

He returned to his office at four that afternoon. Behind his office was a small mobile home in which he lived.

He employed a number of sheriff's deputies who patrolled the county. Monterey County was a good place to live. Not much occurred in Monterey, and Blue was mostly responsible for that.

Blue and Jim had coffee and discussed their solitary murderer. They had police forensics and federal marshals to help them, but it was up to Jim and Blue to uncover the evidence.

In his mobile home, Blue laundered and pressed his uniform, polished his shoes, and cleaned and loaded his weapon.

He left the sheriff's office at five in the morning and stopped at a diner for breakfast. He was looking for someone described by forensics as a connoisseur of murder. He was back at his office that afternoon. He managed the business of sheriff well. A deputy took over patrol of the county. Blue made phone calls, typed some letters, and managed his office's books. He had some county residents with marital disputes he had to look into, and there was a shoplifting at a mall he wanted to investigate. It was business as usual in Monterey County. People went about their business. Farmers farmed. Blue answered calls from upset citizens.

He was back in his trailer by five that afternoon and read until seven. He enjoyed fiction, especially action-packed detective stories with heroes and good endings. He watched TV until eleven.

At five the next morning, he headed to a diner for breakfast and read the paper while eating his eggs. He saw people from different parts of the county who would tell him what was going on. He was hoping to get some information about the murderer.

He left the diner at seven, and at noon, he was once again having a solitary lunch at the rock quarry. At three, he was back at his office to return some calls.

In his trailer home, he checked out his uniform, cooked supper, read, and slept.

He was a former warrant officer in the army. He had retired after twenty years and became sheriff to keep the peace in Monterey County, where not much happened on his watch. He had a solid view of people and knew things. Most people worked and observed the law. But others broke the law. And the murderer was out there among them.

This was all during the Cold War. He believed most leaders were well meaning. There was a stalemate that risked total war. There was Vietnam and keeping the lid on the deep freeze.

He got a call when he was in his squad car. A dispute was brewing in Salinas. A couple was refusing to pay rent. He decided to answer the call. He got them to promise to do so in a week.

He returned to his trailer at lunch after patrolling the coast. A deputy took over his patrol. He listened to the news about the war. People upheld the conflict they waged.

He spent the afternoon at his desk and took over patrolling duties at three. Once a week, he took a night patrol.

At five the next morning, he was having breakfast at a diner when a customer asked him, "What's new?"

"Not much," said Blue.

He read the paper and resumed patrol. He asked vagrants their business.

On the weekends, Blue worked in his garden and mowed the grass around his office.

It was getting to be fall. There was a touch of frost.

He went to church on Sunday. He was a Methodist.

Monday morning found him on patrol again. He had breakfast out by Fort Ord. He drove to the southern part of the county. He noted the traffic.

He knew a lot of people in Monterey, but he was looking for one in particular.

36

Hank and Mabel pulled into the parking lot of the Seaside Hotel. They asked for Dell at the front desk and were soon knocking on his door.

"Hello to both of you," Dell said with a grin. He invited them in.

Mabel sat while Hank stood.

"We've spent six months canvassing Tahoe, Fresno, and Frisco," Mabel said.

"We'll let you know what we have," said Hank.

"Scotch or bourbon?" Dell asked.

Hank and Mabel took scotch while Dell poured himself a bourbon.

"We're isolating a killer, the third protagonist in our murders," Dell said.

"We've been to Nevada and Arizona as well, Dell," said Mabel.

"What do you have?" Dell asked.

"You wrote an essay on a paramilitary figure. It fits in, Dell," Hank said.

"Phil's honest," said Mabel.

"But he's high handed," said Hank.

"We're going to see Blue now. We're staying at the Best of the West hotel."

Dell escorted them out. "I'll see you again tonight or tomorrow," he said.

Dell had been at his typewriter all morning. It was October. He smoked and tried to organize himself. Events were forthcoming.

He shaved and dressed. He headed to the hotel bar for a beer. He had been in the hotel for five months. He could exonerate Phil, but he still hadn't found the murderer.

At five, he returned to his room. Hank and Mabel were coming by at six. They planned to go to the German restaurant for dinner with Jim.

The food was good. They all enjoyed dinner.

"We have a composite of our suspect," Dell announced. He held up the composite. "Jim is putting together the forensics."

"We should have something, Dell," Mabel said.

"I can see everything at *Argo's*," Dell said. "Hank and Mabel were in the background while I fronted the establishment."

"We have your assassin, Dell," Mabel said.

Dell was silent. His view was accepted. Jim spoke.

"McDuff will be here tomorrow. He mentioned he would stop by."

Back at Dell's room, Dell mixed drinks for the group.

"We believe our suspect is in Burt's organization."

Dell agreed.

"I know so many people. We have the background. There is an idiosyncrasy. Let's have a few more drinks and discuss our suspect in Monterey," Dell said.

"We have a paramilitary type," Mabel said.

"I think Phil runs a better magazine than we thought," Dell said. "His magazine stirs up antipathy. I haven't ruled out something else going on clandestinely that surrounds Phil, however."

The four sat and discussed Monterey. The coast was a rocky point that formed the peninsula and Monterey Bay. They mentioned Barbary.

"Dell, Hank has a photo album of last year. It might give us a clue to the whole thing," Mabel said.

Hank, Mabel, and Jim left at eight.

Dell was alone with his thoughts. He had his reservations.

The next morning, he had breakfast at the restaurant. By the time he got back to his room, everything was in order. His bed was made, and there were fresh towels in the bath. The hotel staff took good care of him. They thought he was the house detective.

He opened a beer. He smiled. He believed they were on the right trail. He had a notebook in which he had written all the facts he had about the case.

They could look at things in retrospect. He watched TV. He smoked a pack of cigarettes and drank beer. They were looking at their suspect.

Pat Jorgensen worked narcotics with the Monterey police. He followed the traffic in Monterey, which was a seaport, and he worked closely with the Coast Guard, which tried to capture smugglers. Pat combated drugs and was on good terms with Blue, the county sheriff.

Pat was looking for a kingpin, someone he thought was a member of a foreign cartel. Jim came in. They discussed what was known. Jim said, "I'm looking for someone with a military background."

Jim needed Pat's help. Pat was not popular, while Jim was liked, but such things went with the job. Pat was effective. He followed the traffic. It could be a foreign cartel. Pat was straight with Jim. "The military is investigating drugs in the area," said Pat. "I can give you one or two names."

Dell was in his room when Jim and Blue came by. They discussed the murders. Jim was still looking for a punk, while Dell was sure it was a paramilitary type. They agreed to get McDuff involved.

At eight that evening, Mabel and Hank arrived. Hank had a stack of photographs.

"I take photographs of interest," said the photographer.

"This might give you an idea of what we are looking for," Mabel said.

They talked for an hour as Dell went over the photos.

"Our suspect remains in view. He's part of Phil's organization," Hank said.

"We're narrowing it down," said Mabel.

"McDuff will be here tomorrow," said Dell. "Let's give this a week. Why don't you take a few days off?"

Dell was up at five the next morning and had breakfast. He drove to Salinas and was back at noon. He drank beer and worked on his story. He smoked. He read some of an Honoré de Balzac novel and had dinner at the restaurant, followed by drinks in the bar and conversation with people there.

He awoke at seven the next morning, showered, shaved, and dressed. After breakfast, he waited in his room for McDuff. He planned to present McDuff everything that they had.

At eleven that morning, McDuff knocked. "What do you have?" he asked Dell.

"I have a murder in Monterey and an indictment against Phil," Dell said.

"Please proceed," McDuff said.

He asked for a few days.

"We need to contact the feds," McDuff said.

38

Jim, McDuff, Blue, Mabel, and Hank gathered in Dell's room, drinking and smoking on a Thursday afternoon.

"We're set for Saturday afternoon," Dell said.

The authorities had been informed. The local police stood by.

"Let's review what we know," Dell said.

"Danielle Philips was found dead near Salinas last year, on July 4," Mabel said. "We were running a sting on Phil."

"Our purpose was to penetrate *Argo's* and serve an indictment against the magazine," Hank said. "There were several charges of local and inter-state violations."

"I was asked to stand by as federal prosecutor," McDuff said.

"It was Danielle's murder that got us involved," Jim said.

"She was found with several stab wounds," Blue said.

"These are the events of a summer ago. I was commissioned by Phil to write articles on Indochina," Dell said.

"We were simply to examine the magazine and indict it," Mabel said. "The murders happened later."

"I was in conversation with Phil at the parties to disprove the allega-tions," Dell said. "Phil's a powerful person who manages one of the most lurid and controversial periodicals in print, but his personal demeanor and his accounting for his activities convinced me that I can say he's not guilty."

"We may add one or two murders since a year ago. The charges against Phil were racketeering and drugs and prostitution," Blue said. "Did you find evidence of that?"

"I didn't," said Dell.

"Let's relax for the afternoon. Tomorrow's Friday. We move on Saturday afternoon," Hank said.

They discussed the country and the Cold War and the war in Vietnam. They talked about Monterey with Jim and Blue, the locals.

They had hamburgers for dinner at VIP's and found a bar after that.

Dell was home by ten.

On Saturday, at noon, Hank and Mabel knocked on Dell's door. Jim, Blue, and McDuff arrived shortly after. "I want to be in on the finish," McDuff said.

"We're looking for a paramilitary figure," said Dell. "Jim is a homicide cop. He knows the insidious as well as the rational. He mentions a rich punk. We believed it was just one killer for all three murders, and we were correct. Enrico Di Mayo is a Vietnam vet who was discharged a year ago. He's a local, and his family is well off. The military believes he does drugs, and he's suspected of a murder in Saigon. The FBI arrested him an hour ago. Di Mayo worked at the White Glove in the kitchen. He's been charged, but not Phil. I'm pleased we've nailed Di Mayo."

Hank and Jim asked a few questions, but they were pleased.

"Who figured Di Mayo?" McDuff asked.

"Hank and Mabel covered the White Glove," Dell said. "They matched a composite drawing with one of Hank's photos. Di Mayo stabbed Danielle. He traveled to Tahoe and killed Katie. We have forensics to prove this. He killed Heather. There was an undercurrent to so many allegations. These were the charges against *Argo's*. Di Mayo is the leading figure among others in this undercurrent."

The group relaxed.

"I'd like to see Phil," Dell said. "I'll tell him he managed this well. Di Mayo was blackmailing him."

"We have the allegations," said Hank.

McDuff concurred.

The group rested Saturday afternoon.

At three, they drove to the White Glove in downtown Monterey and were seated.

"The FBI's been by," the maître d' said.

They ordered dinner.

"Di Mayo worked nights, and Phil dined her frequently," Dell said. "Di Mayo threatened *Argo's*."

"Di Mayo has known drug connections," Mabel said. "We identified him through the composite."

"We have him," McDuff said. "Our work in Monterey has been a success."

Hank talked with Jim. Blue was silent.

"Is this your case?" Blue asked Jim.

"Yes," said Jim.

They sat at their table and ordered drinks. They left the White Glove at five.

They sat in Dell's hotel room. A few played cards. They drank beer. McDuff talked with Blue and Jim. They had achieved the success they had bee after for a long time. Hank and Mabel talked with Dell.

"You stood by this for a year, Dell," said Hank.

"Yes," said Dell. "We can give *Argo's* what is due. We must follow up with what we have."

The group was silent.

The party dispersed. McDuff was on his way back to Stockton. He could prove the allegations and make an arrest.

The next afternoon, Phil and Candy welcomed Dell, Hank, Mabel, Blue, and Jim as Mark served drinks. Jonah was there as well.

"Thank you, Dell, for your service," Phil said.

"We have Di Mayo and his accomplices under lock and key. Federal charges are pending," Dell said.

"Your magazine is protected by law. You are free to engage in your business," Mabel said.

"You did well, Dell, with your writing," Phil said.

"Thanks," said Dell.

"Di Mayo wanted to blackmail me by threatening to destroy the magazine, and they wanted to blackmail the salon as well," Phil said.

"Di Mayo was a ruthless manipulator," Hank said.

The HoneyBees performed, and Jonah sang.

"Sometimes, we have to allow events to proceed to unlock a case," Blue said. "Several deaths occurred. We didn't know who Di Mayo was."

"Sheriff," Phil said, "it was Danielle's death with which Di Mayo announced himself, but Tory and I wouldn't give in."

Mark and Chico were told they were no longer suspects. Chico was told to decamp.

"It's always the obvious until the truth surfaces. This was the evidence," Jim said. "Di Mayo's been charged with murder and conspiracy."

"I never thought your indirect approach would yield Di Mayo, Dell," Phil said. "Thank you."

They had lunch and drinks. Phil played host.

The reception came to a conclusion. Blue and Jim said good-bye, and Dell, Hank, and Mabel returned to Dell's hotel.

Back at the hotel bar, the bartender asked them if they had been in the newspaper.

"Yes, we were," said Dell. "We solved the murders."

The bartender lit Dell's cigarette and served them fresh beers.

"We're going home," Dell told the bartender.

Dell thought of the case. Several people had been arrested with Di Mayo. They had constituted a Monterey drug ring.

Hank, Mabel, and Dell were seated in the café, all in uniform. They enjoyed dinner and returned to Dell's room.

"Thanks for your photos, Hank," Dell said.

"Thanks for your composite," Hank said, "and for sticking with the case no matter what other people said."

"We're leaving tomorrow, Dell," Mabel said. She was returning to Salt Lake City, as Dell was, while Hank was returning to St. Paul.

Hank and Mabel left for their hotel. Dell was left alone in his suite. He would see Frank in just a few days in Salt Lake City. Frank and McDuff had stood by him. Di Mayo was in custody. *Argo's* was still in business. Sandberg sat up late.

He left the hotel the next morning. All was quiet in Monterey.

40

In June 1972, Phil was a vindicated publisher of a national magazine. Dell was back in Salt Lake City, working closely with Amanda and Mabel as bailiffs under Frank's supervision.

In California, Blue had returned to patrolling his county. A federal case had ended with multiple arrests. Blue stopped by the East Commune. He wished them well.

Jim had returned to homicide with the Monterey police and was assigned another red ball—San Francisco's Zodiac killer.

Di Mayo was charged with a murder in Saigon. He was addicted to skag and was a drug gang leader. Forensics proved Di Mayo had killed Danielle, Katie, and Heather.

Chico, Mark, and Tory were no longer under suspicion, and Phil had proven that he hadn't been a crime boss.

US Marshal McDuff was at work in Stockton.

Dell smiled at all the memories, including the writing he had done. He planned to write more about Indochina.

Frank and McDuff had stood by him. That's what US marshals did.

CPSIA information can be obtained
at www.ICGtesting.com
Printed in the USA
FSOW01n1503260615
8311FS